Also by Peter Williamso

An Irish Immigrant,

Growing up in Ballybay, and emigrating to find work.

Bloodlines. (Fiction) story of two brothers on Opposite sides during "The N.I Troubles"

Warriors Path (fiction) EMMIGRATION to America in the 1760S

COPYRIGHT 2015

All rights reserved. No part of this book shall be reproduced, stored in a retrieval system or transmitted by any means, electronic, mechanical, photocopying, recording, or otherwise without permission from the author. No paten liability is assumed with respect to the information contained herein. Although every precaution has been taken in the preparation with this book, the publisher and author assume no responsibility for errors or omission's. All characters in this book are fictitious.

Copies of all books by Peter Williamson are available on Amazon and Kindle.

They are also available in U.K local libraries.
Peter can be contacted by email.
pwinks@btinternet.com

CHAPTER	TITLE	PAGE
1	School	5
2	Alexander Williamson	28
3	Pirates	46
4	Young Love	63
5	Leaving Home	82
6	America	106
7	Slave Market	132
8	Privateers	158
9	Travelling West	182
10	Unrest	205
11	War	225
12	Sullivan's Island	243
13	Mary Latimer	263
14	Growing Up	282
15	Warriors Path	305
16	Reunion	326

Chapter 1 School.

Alexander Williamson known to his friends as Alex is eight years of age and attending school on his first day, as he hurried across the long meadow he knew he was late. The master was standing by the school house door with his cane in his hand, Alex knew he was in trouble but he decided to bluff it out.

"Madain Mhath Master", (good morning sir)

Before he had a chance to take evasive action the teacher began beating him across the back and shoulders with the cane, as he administered the punishment he kept repeating.

"English! We only speak English in this school, now take your place in the class"

Alex was not really hurt by the cane, his father Robert kept a switch made of birch at home which he used regularly to administer punishment on him and it was much more painful than the Masters cane. He was beaten regularly with it if his chores were not properly carried out. He took his place beside the only other Presbyterian boy Bertie Millar, the rest of the class were Church Of Ireland, and both of them were privileged to be pupils as the school was funded by Lady Anne Dawson for Church Of Ireland children only. As payment for their education both boys had agreed to work on his Lordships estate for free

English was the second language for most Presbyterian tenant farmers and their families, they hailed from the Scottish lowlands and Scots Gaelic was their native language. Alex was fortunate that his mother Eliza Latimer and her family came from Yorkshire in England, she had refused to learn the Gaelic, and so English was mostly spoken in their house. His father continued to speak Scottish Gaelic to everyone's annoyance, so the rest of the family were forced to speak in both languages. Most of the local farmers preferred Gaelic. After school Alex reported to Tommy Swift the head groom in the stables at Dartrey Castle, Tom led him round to the back door of the kitchen where he was given some food. He was then put to work cleaning and polishing the family coaches, he paid particular attention to the pony and trap favoured by the master Baron Dartrey, who was also known as Lord Thomas Dawson used the pony and trap every day to carry out an inspection of his demesne. Alex also helped the junior grooms to clean out the stables and polish the brasses. The Baron kept a stable of five thoroughbred brood mares, and twelve draught horses for carrying out the heavy work; pride of place went to his Lordships thoroughbred stallion who was treated like royalty, in addition he kept four heavy bullocks which were used for ploughing the land and dragging the felled mature trees to the sawmill located behind the yard. Occasionally a member of the family would visit the stables, the workers were required to stop what they were doing and stand with bowed head, if they were asked a question they could answer but under no circumstances could they lift their eyes to look at the questioner. If he was no longer needed Alex would be sent home about six o'clock. He removed his boots and ran the five miles home to Derrycrenard in his bare feet .On arrival his mother sat him down in the kitchen with a bowl of champ (mashed potato and spring onion) and a mug of buttermilk, he devoured the food in minutes. After eating he went in to the orchard and found the sow he drove her back to the sty and fed her, the pig was his responsibility. As Alex had already eaten he helped his mother to dish out the food to the rest of the family, he had two brothers Robert Jnr aged 22 and William 18 his two sisters were Jane 15 and Lizzie aged 13. Both the girls worked as domestics in the castle, Lizzie had been kicked by a horse when she was ten and the blow had fractured her hip leaving her with a bad limp, she was never allowed upstairs at the castle where she could be seen by the family. The two brothers worked in a corn mill owned by James Swan, it was located two miles distant at Swans Cross. After eating their food all sat around the turf fire and Eliza read from the bible, the family were Presbyterian seceeders but unlike a number of their neighbours they were not fanatical about religion. Grandmother Jane Williamson nee Marshall ruled the house with an iron rod, she had spent years raiding on the Scottish borders with her husband James, she was now in her seventies and spent her days at the spinning wheel.

Robert Williamson was born in 1690 into a reiver family who had their home on the outskirts of Sanchar in the English- Scottish border region. His father James was a member of a group of families, Dixons, Elliot's, Wylie's, and Marshalls who made their living robbing and pillaging from aristocratic estates on both sides of the border. The families owed their allegiance to the Gunn clan who believed that all property was common, and that it was the law of nature. When he was twenty Robert accompanied his father and two other drovers to drive a herd of some fifty stolen highland coos south across the border. Travelling by night using little known paths they arrived in Garsdale, Yorkshire where they handed over the coos to Thomas Latimer, estate manager for Sir Thomas Dawson in return he paid them fifty guineas. They spent the next couple of days resting the horses and catching up on their sleep during this time they were looked after by Latimer's daughter Eliza. She was a very pretty young woman in her early-teens; she impressed the drovers by her hard work, waiting on them hand and foot, in addition to carrying out numerous other tasks around the farm. Robert found himself spending more and more time in her presence and she seemed to enjoy his company, she encouraged him to help her with the chores. As they were about to return home Latimer informed James that the master wanted a meeting with them at the hall, he led them up to the kitchen where Sir Thomas Dawson was waiting. He informed them he would not be buying any more cattle as he had just purchased a substantial estate in County Monaghan Ireland and planned on taking up residence there shortly.

Included in the purchase was a title hence forth he would be known as Lord Dawson. His family and all the staff would be accompanying him; he was now looking for hard working tenant farmers who might be prepared to move to Ireland and work his farms, he had several waiting for new tenants. In particular he had a nice 10 acre plot in the town land of Derrycrenard, this was good arable land and he was prepared to offer it to James for three pounds per annum. There was a modest little house on the plot and it was his if he wanted it. After a lengthy discussion James declined the offer but Robert asked if the offer was available to him. Dawson was unsure as he was very young, but after James vouched for him saying what a hard worker he was, he finally agreed to let him have the farm on the same terms.

Just prior to leaving the Dawson estate Robert sought out Eliza and informed her of the agreement he had reached with her master about the farm in Ireland. As she would be travelling there with her father she gave Robert permission to call on her and if her father agreed they could become betrothed. The four men left just as it was getting dark; they still used little known lanes as their small agile shoeless horses called hobbies were most suited to this type of terrain. Having arrived just outside Gretna as the dawn was breaking, they found themselves in a small picturesque valley surrounded by trees. James called a halt to rest the horses and prepare some food. Now that he was back in Scotland he felt more secure and set about lighting a fire to make a pot of stirabout. The four men were sitting around the fire eating their food when two shots rang out from their front, the smoke from the Brown Bess flintlock guns clearly indicated they were being fired on by two weapons. The four drovers were armed with flintlock pistols and swords which were useless at the distance their attackers were firing from. After the first volley there was a short silence then a voice called out.

"Williamson we know you have a purse of gold coins, payment for the coos you stole, throw the purse over here and you may go on your way in peace"

All four men took advantage of the lull to load their flintlock pistols and the two drovers crawled into the trees behind them and began circling towards their ambushers. James called out,

"Let us leave peacefully and I will leave the purse behind me on the ground"

"We don't believe you, bring it to us with your arms raised above your head"

He knew the drovers would not yet have got into position so he decided to obey their instructions and buy some more time. He called out quietly to his son to keep his head down as he intended to follow their instructions, his son begged him not to show himself. James gingerly raised himself to his full height both arms raised above his head in his right hand clearly visible was the purse with the coins.

"You must meet me half way he called out"

The thieves considered that they would still be out of pistol range so they agreed to his request. They stood up and started moving forward holding their weapons at the ready in the half cock position. It was obvious from their appearance that these two were moss troopers, rogue volunteer militiamen out of Carlisle, they were not wearing their scarlet Kersey coats and were hatless, but they were recognisable by their black stockings, leather shoulder belt with cartouche ammunition box attached. Around their waist was a belt with a scabbard containing a long pointed bayonet. James was almost within touching distance when the drovers crashed out of the trees dirk in hand, they were unable to use their pistols because of the risk of hitting him. Both men were experts with using their traditional blades and the two militiamen were speedily despatched, but not before one of them got off a shot which hit James in the throat andsevering the top of his spine. Robert came running to his father's aid but it was too late he died in minutes clasped in his sons arms. The militiamen were dragged into the woods and buried deep with their accoutrements. If their bodies should be found there would be a hue and cry throughout the border area, if they were not found, they would be posted as deserters. James's body was loaded on to the pack horse and they started off for home. Both men and horses were exhausted when they got to Carron Bridge but they pressed on for home arriving in time for supper. Robert entered first and his mother took one look at him and realised something was wrong,

"Where's your da?

"We were ambushed by the militia near Gretna; my father took a ball in the throat which put paid to him"

His mother's legs began to buckle and he had to rush and embrace her to prevent her falling, he gently sat her by the table and told her everything that had happened. Jane was no stranger to violent deaths and she soon pulled herself together, she knew she had work to do, preparing for a wake, and the burial of her beloved husband. James was buried on a cold wet day in the grave yard at St. Brides Kirk burial ground, the local reiver's attended in full regalia their armour polished and gleaming. Members of the Williamson family and the Gunn clan came from miles around to say their farewells to a brave compatriot. The following day there was a meeting of the immediate family and Robert told them about the offer from Sir Thomas Dawson of ten acres of good land in Ulster at a rental of three pounds per annum. He had spoken of it to his mother and told her he intended to take up the offer as he had no wish to join his brothers down the mine, she informed him that she too would be going with him. His uncle Patrick agreed to supply him with two sturdy pack horses in exchange for the small family cottage. A farewell celebration took place that evening and the following morning they left, each leading a pack horse loaded with everything they possessed in the world.

Robert had fifteen pounds on him, his share of the money they received for the stolen coos, and he paid the ferryman in Stranraer ten shillings to take them across to the coast of Antrim in Ireland. They spent their first night in a cave with a number of other travellers and set out for Monaghan early the following morning. They spent the following night in Armagh town with a cousin of his mother James Marshall, he made them welcome and replenished their depleted supplies at no cost. The following day they entered Monaghan town and took the road to Clones, on entering Rockcorry they were directed to Lord Dawson's estate. Robert and Jane entered through the large ornamental gates and proceeded to the stable yard, they were awestruck at the sight of Dawson house, several steps led up to a beautifully decorated oak door. There were so many windows they could not count them all, and each one contained glass of the finest quality. A man approached them from the stable area and asked their business he spoke Gaelic, Robert informed him that Mr Dawson had offered them some land to farm in Derrycrenard and they had travelled from Scotland to avail themselves of his offer. The man informed them he was Joe Duffy the estates manager for Lord Dawson then he asked them to follow him to his office behind the stables. When they were seated in the office he produced a document from a drawer and passed it to Robert it was written in English, he returned the document saying neither he nor his mother understood English. Duffy then informed them it was a deed allowing them ten acres of land for three life times at an annual rent of £10 paid in advance, he also informed them that his Lordship would review the rent annually, if these terms were acceptable they should make their mark on the document. Robert pointed out that his father had been offered the farm for three pounds per annum by Lord Dawson.

"Duffy replied that times had changed and they had a number of people wanting this farm, they could take it or leave it and return whence they came".

Margaret and Robert made their mark and handed over the money, a copy of the deed together with a map showing the boundaries of the land was passed to them. The manager then passed on a message from his Lordship that if any of his animals went missing their farm would be the first place he would come looking, and if any of his property was found they would both be hanged on the gallows at Swans cross. Prior to departing Robert enquired after Thomas Latimer and was informed that on arriving in Dartrey he was granted the tenancy of a farm of land in Closagh for services to his Lordship, the land was adjacent to his own so they would be neighbours. A local stable hand was instructed to take Robert and his mother to their new farm; they travelled along a rough path surrounded by full grown ash and oak trees, many Rhododendrons in a variety of colours grew in abundance along the route but as it was late June the flowers were dying off. They left the trees behind and came onto a path with a hedge on both sides this climbed gently until they came upon a dilapidated single story cottage. The stable hand departed with a wave of the hand leaving Robert and his mother to admire their new home. The thatch on the roof was in poor condition, the window shutters were broken and hanging by a thread some were lying on the ground. The single front door had broken from its hinges and was lying on the ground, the interior consisted of two rooms one of which had an open fire place. The interior had been used by animals for shelter, and excrement covered the floor. Margaret looked at her son in despair,

"It will take us weeks of hard work to make this hovel habitable, perhaps you should send for your brothers to come and join us without delay"

Robert gathered some kindling to get a fire going while his mother with the help of some farming tools managed to remove the majority of the excrement from the floor. After consuming a bowl of stirabout each they managed to fasten the door and shutters temporarily. They brought the horses inside to protect them from the numerous wolves wandering the woods looking for prey, that night the horses and people kept each other warm. Early the next morning Robert set off in search of the town land of Closagh, he carried his flintlock pistol primed and at half cock at his side he also had his father's sword, he had been warned that there were bands of Raparees (Bandits) scouring the woods looking for innocent victims to rob. At the end of the lane he came upon a fairly large lake he followed the shoreline for twenty minutes when he spotted a farm house high up on a hill. As he entered the yard he spotted Eliza walking towards the house with two buckets of water which she had just collected from the well.

She spotted him and put the buckets down, then hastened towards him.

"Goodmorrow Robert I am pleased to see you"

He picked up the buckets and they walked up to the house. Thomas Latimer was sitting at the table eating his breakfast he stood up and asked Robert to join him, which he did. He told Thomas about the poor state of the farm house and that a lot of work would be needed to make it habitable, and also to prepare the land fit for sowing crops. He asked him if he would write a letter to his brothers to come and join him, he would allocate them both two acres of good arable land for their living. The letter was written without delay and Thomas offered to ride into Monaghan town and post it. Eliza decided return with Robert and help with the work, her father had no objections as he had two sons Richard and William also three daughters Margaret Jane, Catherine, her mother Mary knew Eliza would be well chaperoned by Roberts mother Jane. When they took their leave and started walking back she took the opportunity to point out the farms in the neighbourhood, some of these farmers were neighbours of the Williamsons back in the Scottish lowlands. She also pointed out the best areas on the lake to go bathing when the weather was fine and where the best fish could be caught. Robert was quite happy walking alongside her and listening to her babble on about the surrounding countryside. In no time at all they were walking up the lane to the house there the two women embraced each other warmly and started without delay making plans to make the farmhouse habitable. Robert took the opportunity to get the map out and walk the boundaries, there was much work to be done as the hedgerows and gates were in a dilapidated condition. There was an area of about three acres fit for nothing, the ground was so soft and boggy he sank in it up to his knees. Some of the trees would need to be removed if he was going to put the land to the plough, in his mind's eye he allocated different parcels of land for different crops the soil was good and would produce good yields. The two women were dividing their time between repairing the house and cultivating a kitchen garden to supply vegetables for the house. While they were waiting for their food to be available their neighbours rallied round, for one days labour in the fields they would get several bags of potatoes and various other green vegetables. Three weeks had past when David and James walked into the yard leading their pack horses, Robert and his mother were overjoyed to see them but Eliza was taken aback as years of working down deep coal mines had turn their faces black. She soon become accustomed to their appearance and found their temperament very agreeable. That first night they sat around the fire discussing their plans for the future when they were interrupted by a knock on the door. Eliza went to the door and opened it to a tall young man armed to the teeth.

"I come in peace ma'am; may I speak to the man of the house?

Robert went to the door and beckoned the man in.

"What business do you have with us?

'I have it on good authority you are the son of James Williamson of Sanchar Scotland"

"Aye but my da is no longer above ground, he died in my arms from a ball striking him in the throat fired by two ruffians in uniform who paid with their lives"

"I have heard the story told many times, my name is James O'Hanlon, my father was Count Redmond O'Hanlon he often crossed the shuck and raided the border farms with your father many years ago, now my Da was betrayed and murdered by his own kinsman Art Mc Call"

The men paused now to fill their pipes and Eliza brought a jug of poteen which the men passed around. The three Williamson brothers were consumed with curiosity as to the purpose of O'Hanlon's visit; they kept their 'whisht' and waited for him to enlighten them. He addressed himself to

Robert pointing out that the farm he now occupied was part of the O'Hanlon gang's area of influence. All occupiers of land within the area of Monaghan, Cavan and Armagh were required to pay an annual levy of £1 to support the gang; in return they would be protected from Tories and landlords agents. Robert spoke for the family pointing out he only had £4.10 shillings left and he planned to buy some hens a pig, the rest would be needed for seeds. O' Hanlon took a stiff drink then looking Robert in the eye, he asked him if he would be prepared to ride with him when he next went rustling cattle in the surrounding area. Robert agreed without hesitation but pointed out that he had made a promise not to rustle any of Lord Dawson's animals, should he break this promise he could be hanged at the cross roads. On hearing this O'Hanlon let out a loud laugh, he then informed Robert that his Lordship got a share of the blackmail money and a share in the booty from the sale of rustled animals. They finished off the jug and the reiver went towards the door, Robert invited him to spend the night but he declined saying he preferred to sleep outdoors snuggled up to his horses belly, in the event of an ambush they could fly the trap in seconds. With the Gaelic words *mar sin leibh* and a wave of his hand he was gone. Eliza and the four Williamson's sat for some time staring at the door before James broke the silence,

"Do we have any alternative but to go along with him?"

Eliza then informed them that her father had paid the blackmail, ever since arriving and he has had no problems from the numerous bandits roaming the surrounding forest. With all in agreement they then went to bed.

Chapter 2 Alexander Williamson

Eliza Latimer and Robert Williamson were married in Cahans Presbyterian Church on the 14/02 1730 first born Robert Jnr was born 1732 followed by William 1734 Lizzie 1736 Jane 1739. Eliza had a five year gap before Alex arrived in the early hours of the 13/06 1744, she was in labour for several hours and Roberts mother Jane was tested to the limit of her abilities trying to save both their lives. The baby boy arrived fit and healthy but his mother's life hung in the balance for several days. Eliza gradually got her strength back over the following weeks and Alex meanwhile was weaned on cow's milk.All three brothers had worked hard to make the farm prosperous; they drained two acres of bog and built a comfortable little two roomed cottage for David and James to live in. From time to time two of the brothers would accompany O'Hanlon on a raid to rustle cattle; they never stole more than two or three from a herd of maybe 500 knowing they would not be missed.

The cows were driven to Latton, an area of bog land with only a dangerous narrow track to navigate through it; they herded them into Mullanary Lake where they swam across to a large island in the middle. The island was heavily wooded with good grass and the cattle were kept there until the herd reached about fifty, they were then sent north for shipping across to England, then driven to the meat markets in London. Alex was raised in a harsh environment, he was required to carry out certain duties which were allocated to him by his father, failure to carry out his chores was punished with a severe beating with the birch. His mother was determined he would learn to speak English and get a good education. His grandfather Thomas Latimer undertook to give him lessons in English and Latin, he taught him how to read and write in both languages from an early age. Thomas made a good income from translating legal documents and wills from Latin into

English, most legal documents were written in Latin. He was descended from a long line of Latin scholars and was highly thought of by the judiciary and gentry for miles around. While translating some documents for Lord Dawson he brought up the subject of Alex now eight years old attending the school sponsored by Lady Dawson. His Lordship agreed to recommend the boy to his wife and get in touch with him within the month but he pointed out that as the young boy was not of the ascendant church there could be problems. A week later the schoolmaster presented himself at the Williamson farm, after a long conversation in English with Eliza he was impressed with her knowledge of worldly affairs. He interviewed Alex and pointed out he would have to work hard to catch up with other boys who had started at aged five. Eliza pointed out they had no money and they agreed that the boy would work on the Dawson estate after school for free, he then instructed Alex to attend at nine o'clock the following morning. The next two years flew by Alex with the help of his granddad soon caught up with the rest of his class and passed them by.

He enjoyed his work in the stables at Dartrey Castle home of Lord and Lady Dawson, the work was easy and he was well fed.

He was getting on for eleven years of age when Mr Swift took him to the office of the estate manager for an interview, Alex was sure they were going to sack him. On entering the office Mr Duffy invited him to sit down and went on to tell him why he was summoned. He explained that his lordship's youngest daughter Elizabeth who had been in boarding school in England was coming to live with her parents at Dartrey. She was known for her high spirits and great love of horses, her parents were keen for her to have the services of a stable lad to help her look after her own thoroughbred horses. He would be required to follow her at a discreet distance, her parents knew she would be tempted to tackle jumps which were beyond the horse's capability, should she come off and be injured it was his job to return for help post haste. Alex would be required to make himself available at any time of the day, and prepare the horse of her choice at a moment's notice; he must never look directly at her and must only speak if asked a question. He was now told to return to the stables and saddle her palomino mare for a cross country ride in one hours' time. Alex must choose a fast horse for himself as she will be pushing her horse to its limits, although she was only twelve she was an accomplished horsewoman. Elizabeth arrived one hour later and found her stable boy holding the palomino by the bridle and looking down at his boots. He just caught a glimpse of her fancy riding boot as she placed it in the stirrup then she yanked the reins from his hand and galloped off towards the yard gate. Alex quickly mounted a young colt and galloped after her; once through the gate he soon had her in his sights and settled down to follow at a discreet distance. She must have heard his horse as she wheeled round and galloped towards him. He brought his horse to a standstill and sat there his head bowed waiting for her to approach.

"What do you think you are doing? She shouted.

"Mr Duffy ordered me not to let you out of my sight' he mumbled".

"Look at me when you speak"

"I will not it could cost me my job"

"You are just a peasant boy, and you must do as I say"

"Mr Duffy is my boss not you"

"Duffy works for my father, I could get him sacked"

Alex lifted his head and beheld the most beautiful young girl he had ever laid eyes on; she had a lovely oval face with long curly eyelashes, long ringlets of blonde hair hung down from under her riding cap. She had on, a green tailor made jacket that fitted her to perfection, her white riding breeches fitted like a glove and her riding boots were decorated with ornate scrolls.

"I will do anything you say but please don't get Mr Duffy the sack."

"Ok, race me to the bottom of the field and jump the hedge"

"I will not, you will break your neck"

"If you won't do it Duffy is a goner, come on"

With that she wheeled the palomino around and started at a mad gallop for the hedge at the bottom of the field. Alex wheeled his mount and set off in pursuit, he was still some distance behind when he saw her horse take off and clear the hedge with ease. He tensed himself for the jump and just as he was about to take off his horse jinxed to the right and he went out the side door landing heavily on the ground. He blacked out for several minutes and when he came too Elizabeth was kneeling over him with a worried look on her face.

"Have you broken anything? I didn't realize you were such a poor horse-man"

"You are an idiot; if anything happened to you I would have got the whip"

"You won't say anything when we get back, will you?

Alex had now gingerly got to his feet and checked for any serious injuries, finding nothing broken he asked Elizabeth to fetch his horse which was grazing quietly on the other side of the field. When they were both mounted he took up his position a few yards behind her and they trotted back to the stables. When back in the stables he commenced to rub down the palomino when she grabbed the straw from his hand.

"I groom my own horses; remember that in future, you can clean the tack"

Standing with bowed head he answered

"yes miss"

During the school holidays they went riding every day, after they had left the yard she allowed him to look at her and converse in a normal manner. They became attached and enjoyed each other's company but before long it came time for her to return to college in England.

Alex was now approaching his fourteenth birthday; he had grown into a strong young man and was now expected to do a man's work on the farm. His grandmother presented him with a new suit of clothes with long trousers; he was also given a new pair of boots which he hated.

At the end of September when the days grew shorter it was time to accompany O'Hanlon and go cattle rustling, the time had now come for Alex to play his part in the raids. Robert had been preparing him for this for some time. They had spent many hours in the forest practising sword play, and target practice with his flintlock Pistol. His ability to load and fire the pistol surpassed his father; he rarely missed the target, but could not match him with the sword. When the time came he had cleaned and polished his reiver helmet and breastplate until they gleaming, his grandmother looked at him with tears in her eyes, he was the spitting image of his grandfather James. The three men, O'Hanlon, Alex, and his older brother William left the farm leading their hobbies by the bridle, they travelled along little known paths in the forest. They had elected to rob the Leslie estate at Glasslough, as they passed James Swans sawmill they mounted their hardy little hobbies and continued at a steady trot. These little horses were tireless and where known to travel 150 miles in a single day. As they approached the outer perimeter of the huge estate Molly, O'Hanlon brown and white mongrel dog was sent on ahead, she was trained to locate the cattle without noise or fuss. In just under the half hour she returned wagging her tail and making short excited darts in a northerly direction, the men fell in behind her and sure enough they came across a large herd of cattle. The men went in among them searching for good Scottish Angus beef coos; these animals were docile and easily handled. Having selected three prime animals they manoeuvred them onto the path and set off for Latton. They had travelled less than five miles when there was a sudden commotion and the animals bolted, the three men spurred their horses forward William leading, he observed the lead cow on his knees with a large wolf clamped on his neck. He approached at a full gallop with his sword raised high then when he was within reach he removed the wolves head with one mighty slash, on dismounting he removed the head which was still clamped to the cow's neck by the wolf's dead teeth. O Hanlon arrived on the scene and after examining the animals neck declared that no serious harm had been done. Alex went in pursuit of the other two spooked cows, the first one he found and ushered it back to his brother. All three men went in search of the third one leaving the dog guarding the two animals that they had recovered. Half a mile down the path they heard the sound of a distressed animal and found him submerged up to his neck in a flax hole. These holes were narrow and deep holding five to six feet of water; the cow was threshing about and settling deeper in the water drowning was just a short time away.

"We must stop him bellowing before he attracts attention "said O'Hanlon.

With that he threw himself on top of the animal, reaching forward he used his dirk to slit the animal's throat, the noise abated and the animal settled in the bloody water. The party with the remaining two coos carried on towards Latton, they took paths known only to a handful of people across bottomless bogs until they arrived at Mullinary Lake. They recovered a small rowing boat from the reeds, Alex drove the animals into the water then jumped into the boat and they followed in their wake across to the island. The three rustlers decided to count how many animals were on the island and after several attempts they agreed on fifty four, James informed them he would shortly make plans to move them north before crossing the shuck to England.

On departing the island James headed for Armagh and Alex and William returned home.

That night Robert handed Alex his first mug of poteen and settled down to listen to his story. He was proud of his son and told him he had done well Alex seized the opportunity to ask his da, if he could go on the cattle drive when the coos were moved off the Island. Robert replied that he would think on, as there was no doubt they would need many hands to move a herd that size across boggy swamps. St Jude's day was fast approaching and Robert had twenty ruids (5 acres) ready for ploughing, he was planning to plant winter wheat as a cash crop and weed controller. In return for the work they had done on Lord Dawson's estate during the spring and summer, he allowed them the use of his heavy metal plough and two oxen. These magnificent animals could only work on soft land, it was impossible to shoe them as they were incapable of standing on three legs while the shoe was being attached to its fourth leg. The twenty ruids were completed in seven days then the ground was harrowed before planting the seeds. All available members of the family helped with preparing the soil then the Oxen and plough were returned to Lord Dawson.

It was the middle of October when O'Hanlon turned up accompanied by two experienced highland scots drovers. These two men refused to enter the cabin, they were filthy dirty and the clothes on their back were made from cow skins Margaret wouldn't go anywhere near them as they smelled rancid, they never washed either themselves or their clothes. After consuming a full bottle of poteen they curled up close to the mud wall and went to sleep. Alex observed them eating in the morning, they produced a pigs bladder nearly full of cows blood then mixed it with barley after a good stir they ate it with their hands. William and Alex were to make up the rest of the crew and they left at day break, the two drovers positioned themselves either side of O'Hanlon's horse with the two brothers following behind in full Reiver attire, leading the hobbies by the bridle. When they arrived at the lake they tied their horses up to a sally bush and rowed out to the island, they then spent the rest of the day gathering the animals into an enclosure preparatory to swimming them over to the mainland. The drovers were rowed across by William who then returned to the island, the three men on the island drove the cattle into the water and followed them in the boat; they kept them moving by applying the whip liberally on their backs. On reaching dry land the drovers gathered them into a herd and started driving them north just as it was getting dark. In less than two hours they were crossing the ford over the Dromore River by the sally orchard, they stopped to allow the cattle to drink and the men to get a bite to eat. They drove the cattle through the Leslie demesne without encountering a soul and were in Lord Blayney's estate by midnight. His Lordship was a grand master of the freemasons and spent most of his time visiting lodges in various parts of Ireland and England. During his absences security was lax on his estates, so the rustlers were able to drive the herd through without hindrance. Three hours later they were in the Mourne mountains within sight of Carlingford Lough, this was O'Hanlon's home territory and he led them through an almost impenetrable forest to a large cave capable of housing the cattle and their drovers. A large quantity of hay and fodder had been stored there in order to feed the cattle for several days; after they had been fed the drovers had some food and settled down to sleep. On awakening James left for Rostrevor to arrange shipping across to the mainland, the Captain of the cargo boat was expecting him and a price was agreed after much haggling. A large quantity of hay and straw were packed into the hold of the boat followed by the cattle, the two drovers stayed with them keeping them calm, they picked a spot for themselves and bedded down for the duration of the journey. The captain was an able seaman called Wilfred Shrigley; he was a mixture of pirate and shipper, when the shipping business was poor he would turn his hand to piracy. As O'Hanlon was travelling with the coos the Captain informed him he would be sailing within the hour, he had a favourable wind out of the west and meant to make the most of it. Alex and William stayed long enough to see the boat head out to sea in a south easterly direction towards Holyhead in Wales. They then turned for home. As they would be travelling in daylight dressed as reiver's they needed to stay well away from known lanes, if fortune favoured them they would be home by the morrow.

Chapter 3 Pirates

The crew of six rowed the vessel until it was clear of the land then the captain had the square sail hauled up the main mast, it immediately filled with wind and they were making a steady three to four knots. O'Hanlon made an inspection of the hold most of the animals were lying down chewing the cud, the two drovers were huddled down in the corner fast asleep. He returned to the upper deck and found the captain in his little cabin in the bow. The crew were all busy with their chores so the captain produced a pack of playing cards and a bottle of rum; he invited O'Hanlon to join him in a game of All Fours. He informed Shrigley that he had no money until the animals were sold so the captain advanced him £25 in exchange for two cows; they shook hands on this and dealt the cards. Time passed quickly with neither man winning or losing, after they had drunk the first bottle of rum a second was produced, they were half way through this bottle when the captain raised his head and cocked an ear.

"We are not moving"

Both men rushed aft, and observed the Irish Sea to be as calm as a mill pond; this was a rare occurrence as normally it was racked with high winds and huge waves. The crew were collecting buckets of sea water and dousing the sail, the wet sail would make maximum use of what little wind was present. The two men joined in until the captain called a halt, take in the sail lads and put out the oars , the six crew men got an oar each and started rowing with the captain on the tiller, they made little progress because of the weight of the cargo in the hold. Far away in the distance Shrigley observed another boat off their port side; it appeared to be closing on them despite the lack of wind. He lashed the tiller with a line and having stood up put his spy glass to his eye. He recognised the shape of the boat instantly as butcher Brady's, he was a well-known pirate who operated out of the Isle Of Man. Prior to becoming a pirate he worked in his father's butcher shop in Castletown hence the title butcher, he revelled in the name as it put fear into the heart of his prey . Shrigley counted ten oars on the starboard side and guessed there would be another ten on the port side; he knew he could not outrun them. Brady's boat was manned with captured slaves; he marched up and down a wooden plank which was laid from bow to stern wielding a bull whip, any man observed not pulling his weight felt the lash across his back. The captain turned to find O'Hanlon standing beside him.

"Whose boat is that captain?

"Butcher Brady, and he intends to butcher us all"

"Can we not put up a fight, you have a small cannon in the bow let's use it"

"James are you mad if we fire any weapons the noise will drive the cattle wild, the hold is below the water line and they will ram their horns through the timbers and sink us in minutes. Brady knows what we are carrying so he will try to take us with our cargo intact, all we can do is fend them off with our oars and hope the wind gets up". Within two hours the pirates were close enough to throw their grappling hooks, everybody on the Shrigley boat un- hooked them as quick as they were thrown and tossed them into the sea. The pirates were kept at bay by using the oars to fend them off; neither crew could gain the upper hand. Just as it looked that all was lost James noticed darkness begin to fall, and the sea getting up, he ordered the crew to hoist the sail which soon filled with a strong wind blowing from the west. The captain turned the boat to the south east and was soon out of sight of Brady whose oars were no match for a full sail. He navigated the boat by keeping the North Star off is port bow and as dawn began to break through the gloom he sighted the welsh coast and headed south until he spotted the Menai Straits. The crew now hauled in the sail and took to the oars, Shrigley steered the boat through the straits until he found the isolated little bay close to Caernarvon known only to a handful of mariners. The livestock were disembarked in double quick time, the captain was paid and the boat headed back for the Irish Sea.

O' Hanlon set off immediately for the Cambrian Mountains where he had cousins who would give him shelter in one of the huge caves located in the area. He arrived at nightfall to be welcomed with open arms by his cousin Derek Pritchard, after making sure the beasts were settled and fed the two cousins settled down to a pipe and a bottle of whiskey. It was now for the first time James learned about the cattle plague that was sweeping through England, all movement of cattle between the shires was banned but so far it did not apply to Wales whose cattle had remained clear of the disease. Fat beasts that a couple of months ago were fetching £4 at Smithfield market were now fetching £8. 15s. the bad news was that all roads leading to the Great North Rd we're teeming with rustlers and highwaymen. Derek offered to put six heavily armed men led by himself at £2 a head, and £5 for him, to guard the herd for the remainder of the journey to Smithfield Market. James jumped at this offer as the money he could now receive for the herd was way beyond his expectations; the two men shook hands and retired for the night.

By mid-morning the following day the herd was ready to move, Derek's men were placed two at the point and two on each side, the drovers kept the cattle moving James and his cousin followed behind. It was a leisurely journey allowing the cattle to rest and graze regularly, they needed them to look fat and in good condition when they arrived at the market. As they entered THE GREAT NORTH ROAD just outside of London they were stopped by a platoon of mounted militia led by a pasty faced local magistrate dressed all in black and wearing a top hat, James rode forward to speak to him.

"You have a fine herd of black Angus cattle, where do you hail from?

"Sanchar in Scotland, we heard that your cattle were dying of disease and there was a great demand for healthy cattle, you are no doubt aware that the disease has not affected the Angus breed, we are hoping to sell this fine herd in the market"

The magistrate dismounted and moving among the herd he checked the mouth and nostrils of several cows looking for signs of blood. After remounting he addressed James.

"You need go no further, I will take them of your hands in the name of his Majesty King George, he needs meat to feed his army and navy, I will give you a promissory note for £ 500 here and now"

"I only trade in Guineas replied James"

"Are you suggesting the Kings note is not good? This is high treason and you could hang for it"

On hearing the way the conversation was going Derek called his men to him, they gathered round James their cocked guns aimed at the magistrate, he had a short discussion with the corporal in charge of the militia who recognised the guards as hard dangerous men. He turned around and trotted towards London followed by his platoon and the magistrate scurrying after them. The herd continued towards Smithfield, the closer they got to the market the more bodies they encountered hanging from the gibbet's at the side of the road, it would appear that the poor wretches were hanged in pairs. On arriving at the auction yards they were allocated a holding area for the beasts, word soon spread that there was a herd of fat Angus cattle free of disease and potential buyers flocked to look at them. After James passed his details to the auctioneer he was allocated a lot number and one hour later they went under the hammer, the magistrate was actively bidding but stopped when they reached 10 guineas a head, the bidding continued briskly and the lot was purchased by a London butcher desperate for disease free meat to feed the near starving citizens of the capital. After paying off the auctioneer, his cousin and the rest of the men James was left with 650 golden guineas, he said his goodbyes and headed off alone for the centre of the city.

He found board and a stable for his pony in THE WHITE HART Drury Lane and the following morning after a pleasant evening drinking with fellow travellers he made his way to Barclay and Bevan's bank in the city. Having deposited 600 guineas he was issued with a letter of credit to Dawson's bank in Dublin; on leaving the bank he was accosted by a number of armed men wearing tricorn hats and a variety of different uniforms. He was ordered to stand still and one of the uniformed men pulled his arms behind his back and affixed manacles to his wrists, it was then that the magistrate who failed to buy the cattle appeared, he presented the parish constables with a coin and they retreated leaving only two uniformed constables in charge of the prisoner. The magistrate addressed James,

"I have here a warrant for your arrest on a charge of treason; you will be imprisoned in Newgate prison until the next assizes when you will be tried before a judge and jury"

He was marched to Newgate prison and thrown into a filthy rat infested cell with ten other prisoners. The following day he requested a meeting with the chief warder. He told him how to locate his goods in the White Hart and in payment for bringing them to him he could dispose of his horse and keep the proceeds. He also informed him he was in possession of a fair number of golden guineas and was prepared to pay for a more commodious cell and some decent food. He was later that day transferred into a cell with two gentlemen awaiting trial for counterfeiting coin of the realm. By the time James trial date arrived his two new friends had been tried and hanged. He walked the short distance to The Old Bailey under guard where he was met by a man in a wig who informed him as the charge was treason he was entitled to a defence lawyer. He admitted to the lawyer that he had refused a promissory note from the King for his cattle, and it was pointed out to him that this was an insult to his Majesty King George. As the sentence for treason was to be hanged, drawn and quartered the lawyer suggested he would try and get it reduced to death by hanging. James was led into a noisy courtroom crowded with people wearing white wigs; he noticed his cousin Derek in the public gallery but did not acknowledge him, he was directed to the dock where a clerk read out the charge. The judge barely looked up; he just waved his hand for the prosecutor to present his case, he began by calling the magistrate to give evidence. He gave testimony concerning the accused's refusal to accept the Kings promissory note as payment for his cattle; he pointed out to the accused at the time that this was an insult to his Royal Highness King George and constituted high treason. He and the small troop of yeomen were then threatened with violence by several armed men in the accused's employ forcing them to beat a hasty retreat without the cattle. The corporal of the yeomen was then called to corroborate the magistrate's evidence. James's defence lawyer now stood up and addressed the bench; he informed them that as James had a number of men to pay for their services in getting the cattle to market he needed payment in coin of the Realm, without these men he would have been assailed by the many thieves and robbers on the road and had his cattle stolen. He accepted that his client refused a promissory note but to his credit he had brought much needed meat to the capital which undoubtedly saved many lives. I would beg your Lordship to bear this in mind when handing down your sentence. The clerk now stood before the bench and gave a loud cough whereby the Judge sat up and took notice of the proceedings. He now addressed the foreman of the jury who consulted with his companions.

"How do you find the defendant?

"We find the defendant guilty as charged but in view of the fact that he has supplied a large quantity of badly needed fresh meat to the citizens of London we beg his Lordship to commute the sentence of being hung drawn and quartered, to hanging"

"I must commend the jury for their feelings of pity, but for that I would undoubtedly have sentenced you to the appropriate punishment for a person committing high treason. I sentence you to be taken to Tyburn in one weeks' time there you will be hung by the neck until you are dead. You now have one week to make peace with your maker, may he have mercy on your soul. Take him away"

On his way out he was accosted by his defence lawyer who shook him vigorously by the hand.

"That went well old chap now keep your chin up it will be all over in a week"

The warder escorted him to the condemned cell; here he would receive much kinder treatment and be allowed visitors for the last week of his life. The day following the trial James had a visit from his cousin Derek; he gave him the letter of credit on Dawson's bank in Dublin for safe keeping, he asked his cousin to visit him again in the next few days with a pen and paper. He was back the following day with both items and James wrote out his will naming Derek as his sole beneficiary two warders witnessed his signature. They then settled in a corner of the cell and in low tones discussed an escape plan. It was decided that there was no way he could escape from inside the prison so an attempt would have to be made en-route to the gallows in two days' time. On the Sunday night prior to his hanging James was awakened by the bellman from the Holy Sepulchre who passed the condemned cells at midnight calling out.

"All you that are condemned to die, the Lord have mercy on your souls"

Monday morning he was taken from his cell and dressed in a long white garment and a white skull cap was placed on his head, he was then led to a cart inside the gate where another prisoner was already on board, sitting on a coffin, he took his seat on the second one. When the gate was open the horse and cart set off down Newgate Street with the driver and a single guard sitting up front, only a few members of the public were about as they preferred to congregate in Tyburn where they could witness the hanging, without warning a lone man appeared out of nowhere and threw some foul smelling liquid over the horse, he received a lash from the drivers whip for his audacity. They travelled down Snow Hill towards the bridge that crossed over the Fleet River, half way across they met a lone horseman riding a handsome well-groomed excitable stallion. As the two horses came close together the stallion became agitated and started stamping and snorting despite all efforts to calm him he attempted to mount the mare but the shafts were creating an obstacle. In her attempt to avoid the stallion whose rider had dismounted the mare crashed into the bridge parapet and the rider jumped unto the cart. James spread the leg irons out on the floor two mighty blows from the axe the rider was carrying and the chains parted. He looked up from the irons and observed a mounted Derek leaving The Saracens Head yard leading a thoroughbred mare as he reached the back of the cart one leap from James and he was in the saddle. They turned back up Snow Hill leaving mayhem on the bridge, the cart had overturned with the mare still in the shafts and the stallion was still trying to mount her. The bridge was completely blocked; both the driver and guard were struggling in the river. The two cousins left the city at full gallop via the west gate. They knew that it would be hours before the authorities could mount a hue and cry; they took the old roman road leading to Bristol. After travelling about twenty miles they dismounted at a prearranged spot in a dense wood, Derek retrieved a canvas bag from the dense undergrowth in it was a change of clothes for both men, two flint lock pistols with ammunition, the bag also contained food for the remainder of the journey. After a couple of hours they were joined by the other two cousins who had aided in the escape, it was then that James learned that the foul smelling liquid thrown over the cart horse was urine from a mare in season this explained the stallions behaviour. The following day they crossed the Welsh border and turned north, a day later they were safely home in the Cambrian Mountains where James had the rest of the irons removed. He rested for a week then after saying goodbye to his cousins he travelled to Holyhead where he got a passage to Dublin. The next day he cashed in his letter of credit at Dawson's bank and then purchased a horse and tackle before heading for his home in the Mourne mountains.

Chapter 4 Young Love.

Alex continued working in Lord Dawson's stables; his Lordship was pleased with the way he took care of the estates carriages and work carts. He was coming up to sixteen years of age when Mr Duffy summoned him to the manager's office this time he was not in the least bit nervous as he knew they were satisfied with his work. He sat down opposite the manager who informed him that the master's daughter Elizabeth was returning to live at Dartrey, she had asked for Alex's services looking after her horses and her pony and trap. If he agreed he would receive an extra shilling a week. The manager went on to tell Alex that Elizabeth was returning to Ireland to find a suitor, as she was now nearly sixteen most young aristocratic ladies were married by that age. She was proving to be very fussy and had turned down a number of proposals; she considered that most of the young men she associated with in England were pompous idiots who did not appeal to her one whit. The young men in

Ireland tended to be more adventurous which was much more to her liking, and her father hoped she would find a suitor more to her taste here.

Mr Duffy went on to tell Alex that his wife had died two years past and he was finding life very lonely, he had taken a shine to his sister Lizzie, her lameness did not bother him and he wondered if he could pay court to her. As the Williamson family had despaired of her ever getting a man because of her gammy leg Alex felt that his attentions would be welcomed and promised to speak of it with his family. Mr Duffy (Joe) was afraid his age would be a deterrent as he was twenty years older but Alex felt it would not be a problem. During supper that evening he broached the subject, they all looked at Lizzie and she was blushing furiously.

"He is a kind man and I am very fond of him, I would be pleased to go out with him if mother and father have no objection"

Both her parents gave their blessing and suggested that she brings him to tea on Sunday; Lizzie said she would ask him the next day.

Later that evening there was a knock on the door, when Robert opened it O'Hanlon stood there, he invited him in and made a place for him at the table. He began by placing a purse on the table.

'This is your share of the money I received for the cattle, fifty guineas in gold"

Robert slapped him on the shoulder.

"James that is twice as much as I expected, it will enable me to buy livestock and seeds for the coming year"

Alex enquired of O'Hanlon when they would be going rustling again; he then recounted to them his adventures in London and how he escaped with the help of his cousin Derek. He informed them that as a convicted criminal should he be taken by the authorities he would be hanged on the nearest tree. He informed them that as he had some money in his purse he was planning to travel to the Americas on the first available ship out of Derry. Looking directly at Robert he said it is my opinion that the day of the reiver's is gone, rustling is a very dangerous occupation there are yeomen militia on every road and by-way, they pay good money to informers who are prepared to give them information. He left before midnight his policy being to spend no more than a few hours in any one location as his life depended on him keeping on the move.

Joe Duffy arrived for tea on Sunday afternoon, he was dressed in his best suit, Robert invited him in and the rest of the family who were seated at the table rose to their feet. He took a seat next to Lizzie then the rest of the family took their seats, soda bread and home-made blackberry jam were served up with a large mug of tea. After tea the table was cleared and the family left Joe and Robert alone, they lit their pipes and Elizabeth served them with a glass of home brewed poteen. Joe started the conversation holding up his glass he wished Robert,

"GOOD LUCK"

"Robert replied with 'SLAINTE"

"Now I was wondering if I could pay court to your daughter Lizzie with a view to marrying her come the spring" asked Joe

"If the girl accepts your proposal you have our blessing, you have a fine house and the bad leg she suffers from will not stop her from producing some fine childer in the future, we are not in a position to supply her with a dowry but I don't think that will be a hindrance"

'No! Replied Joe but I would like to pay you back in some way, perhaps you could give me some idea as to how I could do this?

'Well now! The old mother is suffering terrible with the cold, she is getting on a bit now, what we are badly in need of is glass for the windows we have needed it for some time but could not spare the money, if you could see your way to help with this we would be forever in your debt"

"I am going to Monaghan town next week so I will have the glazier pay you a visit, you should have your windows in before the weeks out"

With that both men stood and shook hands Lizzie accompanied Joe down the lane as far as the gate as they parted company he looked at her and said,

"I will be a good husband and look after you"

With that they embraced, Lizzie was so happy, the fact that Joe was so much older than her was not important; he had a good job and a nice house. She watched him out of sight before returning to the house. Joe was true to his word and they became the only house in Derrycrenard with glass windows; all the neighbours came to admire them. Eliza and Joe spent as much time in each other's company as they could, and in due course they became lovers, they decided to get married much sooner than they had planned.

A few days after Elizabeth arrived she sent a message to Alex to saddle her best horse as she wanted to go riding, knowing she was an expert horse-woman he chose a bay gelding for her. On arriving in the stables she approved his choice knowing that this horse had a reputation as a jumper. When she turned her back on him to reach for the stirrup he sneaked a look at her. He estimated her height to be about five foot two inches, a tiny waist that exaggerated her hips, which his father would have approved of as a good child bearing arse. When mounted she looked down at his bowed head, she noted with pleasure despite his age he was nearly six foot with a strong body, devoid of any fat, he was handsome in a rugged sort of way, and would soon be needing his first shave, he had fair hair which nearly reached his shoulders. On leaving the stables she set off at a quick canter, Alex mounted a piebald mare and followed some distance behind. It was mid-afternoon when they entered Dartrey forest and rode down to the edge of the lake, here Elizabeth dismounted and sat down at the edge of the water. Alex dismounted several yards away but she beckoned him forward, he stood in front of her head bowed.

"For heaven's sake will you look at me, I want you to take the horses out of sight into the woods, I am going to swim in the lake so you stay out of sight until I call you"

He warned her that the lake was deep and dangerous as he had swam there many times. She laughed sarcastically, and then informed him she was an excellent swimmer, and if he could swim there it would not cause her any problems.

"Please yourself don't say I didn't warn you, if you get into difficulties don't look to me for help"

With that he walked off into the woods leading both horses, it was nearly an hour before he heard her calling him to return. On arriving back at the lake he found her standing fully dressed but shivering with cold as she had nothing to dry herself with after her swim. He removed the horse blanket of his horse and placed it around her shoulders; she looked into his eyes and thanked him with a smile.

"We must get you home straight away before you catch your death of cold"

She didn't argue but mounted her horse and trotted of back to the stables, on arrival he held her horses head for her to dismount; she muttered a thank you under her breath and quickly headed for the house. When he had not heard from her for a few days he made enquiries of his sister who informed him she was laid up in bed with a severe cold and fever. Over the next few weeks Elizabeth's health deteriorated and she was sent to live with her aunt in Sussex England, her parents felt that the damp misty weather in

Dartrey was slowing her recovery. Alex was worried as he felt guilty for not being more persuasive in his efforts to prevent her from swimming in the cold waters of the lake. His sister Jane kept him informed about her condition, as a chamber maid she overheard the latest news and knew young Alex had grown fond of the young mistress. After several months had gone by and she had not returned he asked his sister if she could find out her address in England, Jane found this out for him on a promise he would not disclose how he had acquired it. The following day he hid away in the hay loft with pencil and paper, he wrote Elizabeth a short letter to say how he felt guilty for not taking better care of her and that he missed going out riding with her. He addressed the envelope and gave it to Bertie Millar who was shortly to accompany Lord and Lady Dawson as their footman, on a visit to see their daughter in England. Several weeks later he was cleaning one of the coaches when Bertie appeared in the stable he had returned from England the previous evening.

In the course of having a conversation about the trip he furtively slipped a letter into Alex's pocket and hurried off to attend his duties. Alex fairly flew up into the hay loft and retrieved the letter from his pocket, it was written in a beautiful neat hand as he held it to his lips he noted the fragrance of roses. At first the words just danced before his eyes but he forced himself to concentrate and began to read the letter. She scolded him for feeling guilty pointing out it was entirely her own doing, had she taken his advice her illness would never have happened. She went on to say how much she missed Dartrey and was looking forward to returning next year fully recovered. In the last sentence she said she missed the pleasure of his company, and wondered if he might be her friend rather than her servant when they next met. She cautioned him that they must keep it a secret as her parents would disapprove of their friendship and he may be dismissed. This part of the letter he read over and over again until he knew it off by heart.

Now that James O'Hanlon had gone from the district a new gang of Raparees came on the scene, they were an evil bunch who would kidnap young members of the families and hold them to ransom. They committed murder and rape stole livestock and helped themselves to the crops when they had been harvested. His lordship had enlisted a company of local militia who he supplied with uniforms and flintlock weapons; he mounted them on swift horses and gave them a bonus for every outlaw they caught and hanged. Alex and his friend Bertie Millar signed up, as his lordship expected all his young workers to do their bit. It soon became obvious that Alex due to the training he received from his father was way ahead of the others in the use of weapons and riding. His lordship observed his performance during exercises and promoted him to lieutenant, to be raised to the rank of an officer was a great honour. The bandits were mainly made up of Belfast riff-raff and led by Jim Murphy a man who had served as a captain in the Kings Own Border Regiment until he was dismissed for drunkenness. The gang had several hide outs and never stayed in the same place for more than a day, as they all had a price on their heads, the local Gentry were offering £50 for every one captured and hanged. Alex was away in the Mourne Mountains searching for bandits when Murphy and a dozen of his cut throats arrived at his family's farm. Robert heard them enter the farmyard and challenged them as to what they wanted, one of the gang dismounted and pointed a pistol at his mother who was sitting in the door spinning. The rest of the family gathered round in a threatening manner, and then Murphy spoke.

"One move from any of you and she dies"

"What do you want of us? Robert shouted at the top of his voice.

"Ten guineas and food as much as we can carry"

"You can have food but we have no money"

Murphy lined the Williamson family against the wall of the house; Eliza was carrying her week old baby boy in her arms, this was the first time her parents had met the newest member of the family. Some members of the gang began bagging up as much food as they could lay their hands on, when they were finished they mounted their horses. Jim Murphy dismounted and walked over to Eliza, without warning he snatched the baby from her arms, she screamed and tried to grab the baby back only to receive a violent blow to the side of the head which knocked her unconscious. Robert Jnr went to her assistance only to receive a pistol ball in his brain. Murphy remounted still holding the baby.

"One of my men will call here tomorrow to collect fifty guineas, if he does not receive it or he does not return I will dash the child's brains out against the nearest tree"

With that the gang rode out of the yard with the booty they had stolen and the tiny baby crying.

As soon as they were out of sight William set off for Dartrey on arriving he rushed to Duffy's office and blurted out the events that had just taken place. When he calmed down it was decided that Joe would return to the farm and look after Eliza, meanwhile he helped William to saddle the fastest horse in the stable, and he set off at full gallop to locate Alex and the troop of militia, he knew just about where they would be. Half way between Blayney and Dundalk he met up with the troop and told Alex what had happened, he figured that the gang would be coming this way in order to get back to the safety of the Mourne Mountains. Four militia men were sent out along different paths to try and locate them, they had orders to take no action but return and report if they found them. One hour later Bertie Millar reported back to say he had located them, they were eating their ill-gotten gains in a wood known as crows island on the Ballybay-Blayney rd. Alex knew the area well as he and Bertie together with some other friends hunted the crows with their catapults when they were youngsters. They had little time to act if they were to save the baby; he could not wait for the other three men to return so the troop set of at breakneck speed for the town-land of Ballintra. Here they dismounted and left their horses tethered to some young trees, they loaded their guns and proceeded with them at half cock in search of the gang. Shortly they came to a shallow brook which ran alongside the wood. Clambering down the steep bank they proceeded to within earshot of the gang who had just consumed Roberts's large quantity of poteen and were in a jovial mood, peering through the bushes the militiamen looked to no avail for some signs of the child. It was obvious the thieves had posted no guards. Alex signalled his men to stay where they were and he climbed up the bank as he crawled towards the camp he heard a baby crying somewhere to his left and he headed there. He found the child still wrapped in his blanket, his crying had disturbed the thieves so they had put him well out of earshot, placing the child in his arms he crawled back to his troop. He handed the baby over to Bertie with instructions to return to his mount and deliver the baby to its parents post haste. The rest of the troop settled down to give Bertie time to get well clear of the area, then on a signal from their lieutenant they climbed the bank and proceeded to crawl towards the bandits, they observed that most of them had fallen into a drunken stupor. Alex called on them to put down their arms in the name of the King but these men knew only the rope awaited them if they surrendered. They jumped to their feet and made a run for the horses, five of them never made it going down under a hail of lead, the remainder mounted their horses before the militiamen could reload. Those of the gang who were still alive were dispatched with the dirk to the throat. One of the militiamen detected a noise in the bushes he signalled the others and they surrounded it; Alex called on the man to come out with his arms in the air which he did.

"What's your name?

He asked the wretch who was still very much under the influence of the drink he had consumed. He got no reply, so he walked over to the camp and picked up a length of hemp which he fastened into a noose and placed over the man's head, he threw the other end over a low branch and ordered his men to take hold of it.

"Now! I need to know where your hideout is in the mountains".

In reply the man spat in his face, on a signal from their officer the militiamen holding the rope took three steps back lifting both his feet just clear of the ground, as his face turned purple and his tongue protruded he struggled violently kicking his legs in the air Alex placed his arms around his waist and applied his full weight to hasten the end. The smell of excrement as the man vacated his bowels told him he was dead so they lowered him to the ground. His lordship sent a cart and two labourers to bury the bandits in the nearby graveyard the following day. The baby none the worse for his adventures was returned to his mother who had recovered from her injuries. Following a mighty wake which lasted all night Robert Jnr was interred in the grave yard at The Cahans Presbyterian church, people of all denominations attended in their hundreds. His lordships militia had now acquired such a reputation as thief catchers and dispatchers, that the Raparees and Tories gave the area a wide berth.

Chapter Five, Leaving Home.

Elizabeth Dawson returned to Dartrey the following year fully recovered, and Alex had her horses groomed and ready she was now seventeen and a fully developed young woman. She had asked her father for Alex to be appointed as her groom and he agreed, he had a high opinion of the young man and fully expected him to know his place and not take liberties with his young mistress. They rode out most days and as soon as they were out of sight of the house they took up a position riding side by side and conversing as equals. One warm summer's day Elizabeth asked him to tackle up the pony and trap; she arrived with a footman carrying a hamper which he placed in the trap. The footman assisted her into the vehicle while Alex held the horses head, she signalled him to join her and take the reins.

"Let's go down to the lake I want to go for a swim."

She saw his look of disapproval,

"Not one word out of you I have come prepared this time."

He pulled up a few yards from the shore, and jumped out to secure the reins to a branch, Elizabeth then alighted carrying the bag and ordered him to remove the hamper and place it on the ground where she indicated. This was the first time he had seen her out of riding clothes, she had a tiny little hat perched on top of her curls a hand sewn silk jacket trimmed in gold also a quilted petticoat which reached down to a pair of dainty brown leather lace up boots.

"You can unharness the pony and take him to a grassy area; I am going to change into my swimming clothes so don't return until I call you"

During Elizabeth's time in Sussex when the weather was fine, she and her cousins spent a lot of time in Brighton at her aunts swimming machine. She had the very latest design in swimwear; designed more for modesty than comfort, a single garment covered her from neck to ankle, only the strongest swimmers could swim any distance wearing it as the garment became extremely heavy when it got wet. Alex heard his name being called and returned to find a blanket had been laid out on the ground with a variety of different foods displayed on it. Elizabeth was already in the water and called out to him to help himself to the food and she would join him shortly. He sat down and watched her swimming with a strong breaststroke to a small island five hundred yards away, she rested in the shallow water before starting to swim back. On leaving the water she walked towards him and retrieved her bag, from it she removed a large towel and commenced drying her hair, she instructed Alex to go check on the pony and not to return until called. When he returned she was fully dressed, she now looked even more appealing after being in the water; she appeared radiant and her pale skin had a healthy glow. She invited him to join her for a feast of chicken and homemade soda bread, between them they soon consumed the food that the cook had prepared.

While they were eating she never stopped talking about her time in Sussex, she described the high society Balls that she attended with her cousins and the famous people she met. Alex listened intently; he couldn't take his eyes of her for one moment and she rambled on, totally oblivious to the look of adoration on his face. Eventually she fell silent and they just sat and admired the beauty of their surroundings, a pair of swans leading two of this year's chicks came swimming up in front of them their dark shadows reflected in the mirror still water. Alex gathered up the uneaten food and tossed it into the water where it was soon consumed by the hungry birds. The time flew by and soon it was time to fetch the pony and harness it to the trap, he loaded the basket and helped Elizabeth to get on board. His lordship was in the stable yard when they drove in, he observed the young couple with a worried look on his face. They were such a lovely young couple but socially a million miles separated them, his daughter was a society debutante eagerly sought after by several of the most aristocratic young bucks in Ireland, while the boy was from tenant farmer stock. The following day it was raining but he noticed Elizabeth spent most of the day in the stables attending to her horses; he approached her and suggested she let the grooms do the work but she wouldn't hear of it. He then approached Alex and sent him off to help out in the blacksmiths shop; Elizabeth's eyes followed him all the way across the yard. His Lordship now made his way to the farm manager's office, as he entered Joe jumped to his feet lowering his gaze.

"Relax man there is no one to see us, have you got a wee dram.?

Joe produced a bottle of home brewed Scottish whiskey and poured two inches in his best glass.

"Pour yourself one and sit down I want to talk to you, have you noticed my daughter and your wife's young brother seems to be hitting it off.?

"I have Said Joe; they make a handsome couple when they are together don't you think?"

"You must let the boy know that there can be no future for him and my daughter replied Lord Dawson, she is destined to marry into the aristocracy and improve the fortunes of the Dawson family."

"I can deal with young Williamson but I have no authority over your daughter, she is the one who is probably going to create the greatest difficulty."

"You can leave my daughter to me, she knows her place, her feelings for the boy are nothing more than youthful infatuation and will soon wear off, I propose we do nothing for a month or so in the hope it will burn itself out."

"That's probably best" Said Joe

With that His Lordship got up and left with a nod of the head. As soon as the weather improved Elizabeth sent instructions for Alex to get the horse and trap ready as she wished to go for a picnic by the lake. After he unloaded the hamper he took the pony to grass and waited for her to call him, when he arrived she was already in the water so he spread the blanket and laid out the food. When he sat down he could see that she was already over at the island, she started the return journey and stood up when her feet touched the bottom displaying only her head and shoulders. Alex now realised she was not wearing her swimwear and she called out to him.

"Will you join me, I will not watch while you take off your clothes?

True to her word she turned her back on him and he stripped naked before joining her in the water, she immediately challenged him to a race to the island and back. He won by a length but she pointed out that she had already done it once and she was tired. Elizabeth ordered him to repeat the swim while she got out of the water and dressed. When it was his turn to get out of the water she left him the towel and turned her back while he dried himself and put his clothes on. While they were eating the food a couple of small forest deer came down to the water's edge to drink, Elizabeth tried to attract them with an offer of bread but they scampered back to the wood. Alex having eaten had stretched out on the ground and despite Elizabeth chattering away dropped off into a deep sleep, he awoke with the feeling he was being kissed, as he opened his eyes she jumped to her feet and ordered him to fetch the pony while she gathered up the dishes and put them away in the basket. Now he was fully awake he realised he must have dreamt about the kiss and they drove back in silence. The following day the weather had deteriorated and it was too cold and wet for them to visit Corravacan Lake, Alex alternated his time between the blacksmiths shop and the stables. Elizabeth always appeared in the stables when he was working there, he thought nothing off it but when he was in her company he averted his gaze from her as he knew his behaviour was being observed. A couple of days later

Elizabeth was informed that the family were to pay a visit to her aunt Agnes at Clonkearney Manor Markethill Co. Armagh , she was instructed to pack her trunks for a three month long stay. They would be there for the hunt ball one of the biggest occasions in Ireland for young aristocratic men and women to meet and form liaisons which sometimes could lead to marriage. Alex spent the next couple of days getting the family coach prepared for the journey, all the harness had to be waxed and the brasses polished, four of the best behaved horses were groomed. Two shires were dispatched on the previous day to await the arrival of the coach at the bottom of Markethill bray on the Belfast coach road; the hill into the town was too steep for the four horses to pull a fully laden coach over the brow so the shires were harnessed to add pulling power, at the top they were unharnessed and returned to Dartrey. The following day Alex was ordered to harness the pony and trap and deliver it to the family as it was needed by the family to get around the estate and to attend services at the Presbyterian Church on a Sunday. He set off at dawn with a saddle pony tied on the back for his return journey, when he arrived in the stables at midday Elizabeth was waiting for him, in the course of assisting him to unharness the horse she slipped him a note, knowing that her father was observing them from across the yard. Keeping his eyes averted he mounted his horse and when leaning down to take hold of the reins he whispered goodbye, she too keeping her head turned away from her father whispered Goodbye Alex. When he was a couple of miles away from the manor he dismounted and read the note, Elizabeth wanted him to meet her the following Sunday evening at Drapers Hill Gosford a local beauty spot. He must tell no one, if her father was to find out he would forbid her to leave the house, he remounted and continued home. The road he travelled was the mail road to Newry it was patrolled regularly by troopers protecting the mail coaches so the Tories and Raparees gave it a wide berth. The following

Sunday Alex borrowed his father's little horse which he had kept from his days as a reiver and rode to Drapers Hill. When he arrived Elizabeth was already waiting for him, she got hold of the reins and tied them to a branch as he dismounted.

"Have you been waiting long?" he asked.

"Not very long, shall we walk through the woods I don't want anyone to see us."

They headed side by side for a gap in the trees the path was rough and uneven, they had only gone a short distance when Elizabeth stumbled on a tree root instinctively he reached out and took her hand, when she recovered her balance they carried on walking still holding hands.

"I've missed you, can we find somewhere to sit and talk"

They entered a small clearing with a large chestnut tree in the middle, they found a clean piece of ground where they sat down together, Alex realised he was still holding her hand

and she seemed happy to leave it there. For the next hour they talked to each other about their dreams and ambitions, about their families the ones they liked and didn't like. They both spoke about how they enjoyed each other's company but that they could never be anything but friends, they came from different worlds he was destined to be a farmer and she would undoubtedly marry some aristocrat selected for her by her father. They returned to the horses after an hours talking, as he helped her into the trap she finally released his hand.

"Can you come again next week?" she asked?

"Nothing will stop me Elizabeth"

They continued to meet every Sunday; they sat under the chestnut tree holding hands and discussing the events of the week. The main topic of conversation among the local residents was the parishioners from the Cahans Presbyterian church's plan to emigrate enmasse to the New World under the leadership of the Rev Thomas Clark. They knew several of the people planning the voyage, and each time they met Elizabeth brought up the subject, finally she got up the courage to ask Alex if they could join the exodus. He pointed out that neither of them had any money to pay for the voyage, and that her father would hunt them down before they boarded the ship. That evening as they parted she reached up and kissed him gently on the lips.

"I love you Alex, and I will never consider any other man to be my husband, will you speak to the Rev. Clark?, if he agrees to take us then when we arrive in America we will get married ,as we will be well out of reach of my father."

He looked at her lovely face with tears running down her cheeks.

"My love, I would be the happiest man alive if you were to become my bride, but the problems facing us are almost insurmountable, during the coming week I will visit the Rev

Clark and discuss our situation, he will recognise what a powerful man your father is and will be afraid of repercussion's should he find out you have absconded with me"

"Please Alex for my sake speak to him, I have been told he is a good man and I feel sure he will try to help."

They parted company with a kiss, this time Alex held her close to him, and she slowly pushed him away before returning to her conveyance. After finishing work on Monday he paid a visit to The Cahans Presbyterian church where he found the Rev Clark in a meeting with the elders. While he waited for the meeting to end he visited his brother Roberts grave and said a few prayers for the repose of his soul. When he heard the clatter of hooves on the adjacent road he knew the meeting had ended so he made his way back to the church. The Reverend approached him and shook hands he knew all the Williamson family as good Presbyterian's but they did not attend church as often as he would like. The report from the last elder to visit their house felt they did not discuss the bible and pray nearly enough.

"Now Alexander what do you want with me?"

"Can we go in the church Sir? I would not like us to be overheard"

They sat facing each other below the pulpit and Alex began to tell him how Elizabeth Dawson and he had fallen in love; the vicar listened without interruption, and when he had finished he took the boy by the hand.

"You must listen to me boy ,The Dawson's will never agree to their daughter marrying a common farm hand, should they find out about your liaison's your life may be in danger, if they didn't kill you they would almost certainly send her far away out of your reach and turn your family out on the street."

"Can I discuss the plan Elizabeth and I put together, she will write to her father in forming him she has gone to visit her

Aunt in Sussex England, it will be several weeks before he finds out that this is not true. With your permission we would like to join your congregation bound for America, we will only have the clothes on our backs but we are both strong and prepared to work to pay for our way."

The vicar replied,

"I can see you have put a lot of thought into your plan but there is one thing you have not considered, the elders in the church will not agree to a young unmarried couple travelling with us sharing accommodation they would consider it indecent, however as you are both of full age there is no impediment to you marrying prior to us leaving for the ship. If you turn up next Sunday evening I will supply two discreet witnesses and perform the marriage ceremony, we are not afraid of his Lordship as shortly we will be beyond his reach."

The following Sunday when Alex turned up at the rendezvous Elizabeth flew into his arms and for the first time they kissed passionately, when they were seated under the tree he told her about the meeting with Rev Clark, if they left immediately in the trap they could be there in an hour in time to get married. She jumped up and pulled him to his feet,

"Let's go! "Hurry up man"

The Pony made good time and when they arrived the Vicar was waiting with the two witnesses Mr & Mrs Wilson, the ceremony was all over in half an hour, Alex had bought a second hand ring of a Gipsy woman it was a good fit. They all sat around and the vicar explained that their ship the John was scheduled to sail from Narrow Water Newry on the 9th of May weather permitting, there was three hundred passengers travelling from Cahans and he estimated they would arrive in New York at the end of July1764. Mr Wilson pointed out that if Elizabeth would help with the numerous children he had eight himself and Alex undertook to dig latrines on the journey they would be fed and clothed as payment for their labour. The immigrants would be leaving tomorrow Monday the 6th May that would give them three days to reach narrow water Newry. The newlyweds retraced their steps to Drapers Hill and parted company from each other, Elizabeth was afraid her uncle would come looking for her if she did not return immediately. They arranged to see each other at the Cahans meeting house at dawn the following morning neither where to say any goodbyes to family or friends. Elizabeth left a message for her uncle to say that she had gone to visit her aunt in Sussex England and would he please notify her father, and tell him she would write when she arrived. Alex left early to walk the couple of miles to the Cahans he could not take the pony as he would have no way of returning it, as Castleblayney was closest for Elizabeth she took the pony and trap, she left it at the stables with instructions for it to be returned to her uncle. The Rev Clark together with the elders who were travelling got the assembly organised and headed off in the direction of

Ballybay, they rested in the town square and local residents supplied them with food and drink. After the rest they travelled to Castleblayney here they were met by Lord Blayney who gave them the use of the stables for a nights rest. Shortly after arriving Elizabeth found Alex she busied herself preparing the children for sleep while he gathered several wooden buckets from the stables for people to use as toilets. When they had attended to their duties they took themselves off to find a secluded spot in one of the hay lofts. They began love making tentatively by shyly kissing and cuddling, but their passion soon became aroused, neither were aware of their role but nature took a hand and they successfully completed their love making. Alex was a gentle lover and his penetration was slow causing Elizabeth little discomfort or pain. After a short rest they repeated their love making this time with more passion, they then snuggled up together and went to sleep. The following morning they both set about helping with their various tasks Alex gathered up and emptied the slop buckets while Elizabeth helped with feeding and washing the numerous children. By early morning they were on their way to New Town Hamilton, some of the elders had gone ahead to prepare for fresh food and drink, they rallied the Presbyterian community to welcome the emigrants.

Back in Dartrey Joe Duffy noted Alex's absence and as no one not even his wife had mentioned that he was sick, he felt it his duty to notify his lordship. When Lord Dawson received this information and having received a letter from Elizabeth the previous evening that she was making a surprise visit to Sussex he felt uneasy. He rode into Monaghan and visited the Dragoon's barracks, here he met with Col Bolger, he told him about the fear he felt that his daughter Elizabeth may have eloped with young Alex Williamson. They were both aware of Dr Clark's exodus from Cahans and they agreed that the young couple may have joined his congregation bound for America. Col Bolger pointed out that they would still be on the road to Newry and if his Lordship wished he would start out immediately to intercept them. The Col knew Elizabeth having met her several times at official functions, in his opinion they would pass through Newtown Hamilton sometime later in the day. He called for the Sergeant Major and ordered him to have a platoon ready to move out within the hour. Lord Dawson returned to Dartrey satisfied that he had done everything in his power to apprehend the young couple. On entering the town square in Newton Hamilton Dr Clark called a rest stop, the local Presbyterians arrived from all directions with food and drink. Alex directed the people to some waste ground behind the houses to carry out their ablutions while Elizabeth helped with feeding the children. As they were preparing to leave the Dr. heard the clatter of a horse travelling at full gallop when it came to a halt he recognised Alex's Sister Eliza, she jumped of the horse and limped towards him.

"Sir I need to speak to my brother it is urgent"

The reverend called Alex to him as he was staying out of sight not knowing the purpose of the horseman, when he came forward he recognised his sister, fearing the worst for his family he asked her about her business.

"I overheard his Lordship telling my husband that he had sent the soldiers after you they are to find you and return you to Dartrey is Miss Elizabeth here?

"I am said Elizabeth, and I am not going back Alex is my husband and I intend to spend the rest of my life with him"

"Eliza you must return now before you are missed, I will deal with the soldiers said Dr Clark, take a different route back and be careful"

They watched her ride out then he turned to Alex.

"Both of you must leave us now and make your way to Bessbrook the minister is a friend of mine and I will send for you when it is time to board the ship"

They moved deep into the woods and continued their journey to Bessbrook, there they met Dr Clarks friend Rev Arnold who hid them in the meeting house. Col Bolger arrived in the afternoon and examined all the adults in the party without success, the vicar assured him the people he was looking for were not with them, not doubting the word of a clergyman he reported back to Lord Dawson. That evening the emigrants arrived in Warrenpoint where the Captain Luke Kiersted had set up his office they formed an orderly queue and when their turn came they handed over their fare of £3, those with no money signed papers of indenture, three years labour without wages for an adult would cover the cost of their fare. The following day after loading linen goods for the American market they began to load the passengers in lighters and rowing them out to the ship anchored inNarrowater. After dark word was sent to Alex and Elizabeth that a rowing boat was waiting to take them unnoticed out to the ship, they attended the Captain in his cabin and signed the indenture Papers without delay. The following morning 10/05/ 1764 the good ship John upped anchor and sailed into Carlingford lough the wind was good, blowing from the south west. The following morning was a fine spring morning and all the passengers gathered on deck to say their good bye to their beloved homeland. There was still some snow on the summit of the Cooley Mountains, blossom was beginning to appear on the trees and the tears flowed like water down sad faces as they called out "Leibh Leat" my beloved homeland. (goodbye).

Chapter six America

The weather remained calm until they reached the Irish Sea where they were met by a violent squall, it became so bad the captain was forced to reduce sail, the sailors hauled in the fore royal and the fore top gallant then the fore top sail, the weather continued to deteriorated, so the captain ordered the jib, main & top royal gallant to be hauled in. They made slow progress as they sailed around the top of Ireland where they turned west into the Atlantic Ocean; sea sickness was rife among the passengers so Alex and Elizabeth were kept constantly on the go helping the wives and children. They were four weeks out when Elizabeth began to feel sick in the morning at first she believed it was sea sickness but then she noticed that as the other passengers got their sea legs her morning sickness got no better. Shortly after, she felt the first stirrings in her belly, but she was reluctant to tell Alex that she was with child. Other women who recognised her symptoms and knowing it was her first child felt they would need to keep an eye on her. They were five weeks out when the Captain was roused from his cabin by the master of the watch,

"Pardon me sir but there is a sail bearing down on us from the starboard side".

"What do you make of her John?

"She is a large square rigged vessel sir, too far off to identify clearly"

"Proceed as normal said the captain, if she appears to be closing call me in a couple of hours".

John returned on deck and took up a position where he could watch the mystery ship which was ploughing towards them with a full head of sail. More and more passengers took up positions at the rail, looking towards the mystery ship, an hour later one of the young men called out she is a British man of war I can see the white ensign. John returned to the captain's cabin and reported the ship closing with them was a British warship. The captain ordered him to strike the top sail as was customary on meeting a warship at sea; they would wait for them to come alongside. Although Britain and America were going through a difficult time they were not at war. One hour later H.M.S Triumph pulled alongside The John and the captains conversed with megaphones, Kierstad demanded to know what the Captain of the warship wanted. He informed him that The Triumph was on her maiden Voyage, having been launched in Woolwich in March; she was a seventy four gun third rate warship and was several men short of a full compliment. He required the captain to allow his press men to come on board to look for young fit men to complete his crew. If they offered no resistance the captain promised not to impress any of The Johns sailors and would allow him to continue unmolested. The Rev Clark was privy to all that was said, approaching Captain Kierstad he informed him he would not stand by and allow his parishioner's to be impressed, the captain pointed out that it was either the passengers or his sailors; if the sailors were taken he would have no choice but to return to Ireland as it would be too dangerous to continue with a reduced ships company. The Rev informed him they could not return as the passengers had sold everything they owned and only starvation awaited them back in Ireland. The Captain raised his megaphone and requested to know how many men were required, the reply came back we will manage with eight. So be it, the reverend said I will line the men up, with that the captain ordered the Jacob's ladder to be lowered over the side. A life boat was lowered from the warship and four sailors embarked each taking up an oar, they rowed to the John and tied up to the ladder. The boatswain's mate climbed the ladder followed by three ordinary seamen on boarding he looked towards the quarter deck and saluted the Stars and Stripes. He passed a copy of the Kings warrant which authorised him to impress any man on board between the age of eighteen and fifty to serve aboard his warships. The captain only glanced at the document as he had seen one before and knew the consequences of refusing to comply with it. Dr Clark had twelve men lined up on the main deck for the boatswain's mate to evaluate; two of the men were immediately discarded as being too old, he enquired if any of the men had a skill only to be told they were all farmers or farm labourers. Alex could see Elizabeth being comforted by some of the women, as he stood head and shoulders above the other men he would certainly be chosen. The boatswain and one of the sailors walked along the bank of men inspecting them while another two sailors walked behind them, two men were quickly discarded as they showed deformity in some of their limbs, and the rest had the Kings shilling shoved in their pocket by the two sailors in the rear. The Boatswain now addressed the remaining eight men.

"You men are now part of the Kings navy, any attempt to escape or refusal to obey orders will result in you being hanged from the yardarm as per Kings Regulations, you can now have a few minutes to say goodbye to your families then climb down into the boat"

Elizabeth flew into Alex's arms kissing him passionately, he whispered in her ear,

"Where ever you go I will find you, they may take me now but they won't be able to keep me, Good Bye! My love"

With that he pulled himself free and walked towards the rope ladder when all eight men were on board the boat headed for the Triumph on pulling alongside they climbed aboard. The impressed men were kept separate from the rest of the ship's crew; they were shorn by the barber then marched to the heads, here they were hosed down with salt water to remove any fleas or bugs they may be carrying on board with them. They were then taken below to the marine's barracks where each man received their uniform consisting of a low cocked hat, pea jacket, and loose canvas trousers tight stockings and buckled shoes. They would not be allocated their duties until the captain had inspected them on the morrow, in the meantime they were shown to their sleeping quarters. At seven bells the following morning the Captain carried out his inspection he looked resplendent dressed in his number one uniform, he had the men lined up below the Quarter deck, prior to inspecting them he had been informed that the men were farmers with no specialist skills.

"You men are now part of his majesty's navy, the finest navy in the world, you will serve on the gun deck where you will be trained to load and fire the twenty eight thirty pound guns, these guns and the gun deck will be kept spotlessly clean at all times. Those of you who are willing to become volunteers will be given the rank of Landsmen seaman and will receive nineteen shillings a month and a share in prize money; you will be required to pay the Purser for your uniform out of your first month. Those of you who don't volunteer will be kept in the Brig when the ship is in dock should you attempt to escape you will be hanged. We will return to Plymouth for repairs and alterations after we have completed the trials, then we will be attached to a squadron and given our posting. Those of you wishing to volunteer will report to the Purser immediately. You will now raise your hats and give three cheers, **GOD SAVE THE KING!!** *God save the king, God save the king.*

All eight men off the John signed on as volunteers and were welcomed by the rest of the crew; to celebrate, the Captain awarded the whole of the ships compliment and extra ration of grog. The eight landsmen now reported down to the gun deck to be shown their duties, an able seaman led them and allocated each in turn to one of the twenty eight guns. Alex found himself part of a gun crew on the starboard side. The gun was operated by a team of six men led by able seaman Graham Woods who hailed from Derby England he was referred to as the gun captain, Graham was impressed by Alex's size and obvious strength, he introduced him to the other four members of the team Ordinary seaman Michael Nagy from Loughborough England, Landsmen Martyn Sparks, Kyle Warner and young Emmet Atkinson the powder monkey. As Graham had been allocated free time to begin training the new recruit he started without delay, they went through the full drill of lifting the lids on the gun ports. Next he showed the recruit where everything to do with loading and firing of the thirty two pound cannon was located and described its function. He explained it was imperative to ram a wet swab down the barrel to douse any fire from a previous discharge, the main charge, gunpowder in a cloth would then be rammed down the barrel followed by the cannon ball, the wad was then rammed home to prevent the ball rolling out, he used the pricker to pierce a hole in the main charge and demonstrated the art of priming with fine powder, they would then retreat twelve feet behind the gun and he would then sight along the barrel before pulling the lanyard. A spark from the flintlock would ignite the powder in the primer which in turned ignited the main charge the velocity and distance the shot travelled depended on the size of the charge. Now that she had a full complement of sailors the Triumph continued with her trials, every aspect of her sea worthiness was tested, the gun deck was inspected every day for its readiness to go into battle. Once a week the first lieutenant practiced a mock attack with a watch in his hand, each gun was timed and ninety seconds was the optimum time to reload after firing. At some time during the trials each new cannon was required to be proofed this involved loading with maximum shot and powder then firing without a ball, no breech rope was attached so the gun could recoil up to fifty feet and this area had to be cleared. The main objective of this firing was designed to remove rust and debris from the barrel; this was the first exercise Alex took part in as a rammer. Because of his height and build he had been chosen to take charge of this important part of the operation, after the gun was proofed it was crack tested then loaded with a ball. In the process of loading the gun it was angled upright to prevent the ball rolling out before the wad was rammed in by Alex, they then lowered the barrel and all hands were required to pull the two ton gun carriage tight up against the ships side. The gun captain now retreated twelve feet behind the cannon and sighted along the barrel, when satisfied he was on target he pulled the lanyard attached to the flint lock this fired the ball with great velocity a distance of approximately 200 yards the distance depended on the size of the shot. The recoil was restrained by the breech ropes to a distance of eleven feet. After the Captain had completed the trials the ship returned to Plymouth for repairs and modifications, Alex received one week's shore leave, he considered it an opportunity to desert and find a passage to America to look for Elizabeth, she was never out of his mind day or night. He was well aware of what to expect if he got caught, he had no money so he delayed making his decision, the day before he was due back on board he met up with

Graham Woods who treated him to a flagon of ale in the nearest bar. They exchanged their stories and Graham sympathised with Alex being separated from his wife, he informed him the Triumph was sailing tomorrow for the Americas to join Admiral Townsend's fleet. Alex now decided he would return on board and wait for his opportunity to jump ship when they reached America.

The Triumph set sail for America with a full crew, the voyage was without any serious incident, the gun crews trained continuously until the Captain was satisfied they could reload their guns in the required ninety seconds. Because of his height and build Alex stood out from the other gunners, he learned how to do all the different tasks and could fill any position in the gun crew. The crew were in high spirits as they anticipated they would be sharing prize money before the voyage ended. Six weeks and three thousand miles later they entered the harbour in Boston on Christmas day. The majority of the crew were granted furlough, in the town;

Graham and Alex had developed a close friendship during the voyage and decided to stick together for safety. Relationships between His Majesty's navy and the citizens of Boston were strained; The King had been imposing unpopular taxes on the population and they were taking it out on members of the Royal navy. Fights between both factions were an everyday event and the sailors were being advised not to get caught on their own. The two friends decided to stay within the dock area and spend the night on board, having discovered a warm friendly pub THE GREEN DRAGON frequented mostly by British sailors the two men shared a bottle of the finest Jamaican rum. Alex asked his mate if he had any idea how far it was to NEW YORK as that was where The John was bound for, Graham had to admit he had no idea how far away it was by land. He put his hand on Alex's shoulder.

"Listen to me my good friend you have no money, no horse or weapon it would be suicide to attempt to travel the roads alone, now the first Lieutenant has let it slip that when we have provisioned we are bound for the West Indies to hunt down and capture privateers and pirates smuggling tax free goods into the Americas, that will mean the crew getting a share in the Prize money".

"I miss her terrible Graham she is the love of my life, and I promised to look after her God knows what has become of her".

"Alex without money in your purse you are doomed to failure, come with me to the West indies and you can have my share of the prize money, I will even desert the ship with you and help you to find your Elizabeth, we will be back here in Boston within the year".

"You're right Graham, it will be hard, but one more year will make little difference".

The following day the Triumph set sail into the Atlantic; from there she entered the Saragossa Sea, the spotters in the crow's nest were changed every two hours lest they get careless and miss a distant sail. The weather was getting progressively warmer each day but the men were kept hard at work improving their capabilities, at cleaning and scrubbing decks. The gunners were only responsible for the guns and gun deck, their only relief from the tedium was when they were compelled to take part in boat and fire drill. After some weeks searching the Saragossa Sea they entered the Caribbean having found no pirates or privateers they headed back for America, as they passed the English Cayman Islands the captain took his ship into the bay at Georgetown and dropped anchor. They had been at sea for five months and were desperate for fresh water and food, the boats were loaded and the cooks and their mates went ashore in search of fresh meat and vegetables, rum was also in short supply and the sailors were grumbling. That evening the captain and several of his officers went ashore to have dinner with the governor, to the crew's surprise they soon returned, when back on board they weighed anchor immediately. There was great excitement among the officers, and all sail was set, an extra man was sent aloft and the Captain spent most of the time marching up and down the quarter deck. It soon became public knowledge that an American privateer the schooner Freedom had called at Georgetown that day, she had hastily re provisioned before setting sail only a couple of hours before the Triumph arrived. The captain was informed that she was fully laden so there was only one place she could be heading for, America, he was now determined to give chase and capture her as it would be a valuable prize. It was early afternoon as they were approaching the Gulf of Mexico when there was a shout from aloft.

"Sail Ho!"

"Where away shouted the Captain"

"Two points of the starboard bow"

All eyes turned to the front of the ship, and within an hour the Privateer came into plain sight on the distant horizon, the Captain conferred with the first lieutenant.

"How long do you think before we come up to her" he asked"

"The guns will be in range by daylight, she is not making good way because of the load she is carrying" replied the Lieutenant"

"I want her, and her cargo intact this will be The Triumphs first prize and the officers and men are sorely in need of some prize money, tonight we will show no light on the mast,come daylight I want to surprize her, we will place an extra look out in the fore yard"

The captain then ordered the officer in charge of the marines to send his best marksmen aloft, they were located in the rigging by midnight; the ships boarding party were to be issued with a cutlass and tomahawk each, and stand ready to board the privateer at dawn. The cannons were to be loaded only with grape shot as he did not want the privateer or her cargo damaged, finally he ordered complete silence on board. It was a long night; the captain never left the quarter deck, just before dawn he inspected the boarding party in the first light. The privateer came into view about eight hundred yards of their bow, they were now well inside the Gulf of Mexico. The Triumph was rapidly closing the gap, when it reached two hundred yards the captain ordered a shot to be fired across her bow. This had the desired effect as the privateer immediately lowered her flag, and reduced sail allowing the Triumph to draw alongside where the captains could converse with each other. The captain of the privateer called across to the Triumph that she was a lawful ship, about her lawful duty, he had letters of marque issued by The Continental Congress of America. The captain of the Triumph then informed him that America was an English colony and did not recognise their authority, he informed the Captain he was sending across a boarding party and if they offered any resistance he would have his entire crew swinging from the yardarm by nightfall. The first lieutenant then led a boarding party of ten experienced sailors and they boarded The Privateer without incident the Captain introduced himself as Willy Connolly. The Lieutenant ordered him to line his sailors up with their weapons placed in a pile on the deck; the men who had been listening obeyed without complaint. As privateers normally carried a large crew it was surprising there were only twelve sailors on board, Connolly then informed him he had been searching for Pirates for six months having captured four ships intact he put a prize crew on board each of them and sent them back to America to be disposed of by the owners of the privateer Robert and Patrick Gilmore merchants of Pennsylvania, the crew were looking forward to a sizeable pay out in prize money when they returned. The crew of the prize were locked up below before the boarding party did a stock take of the cargo; it consisted mainly of rum and molasses items which had been heavily taxed by the King and would show a huge profit in Boston. On opening the ships brig they discovered two slaves in irons; they spoke not a word of English but looked as though they had been well cared for. The Lieutenant returned to the Triumph accompanied by two sailors and six of the privateer's crew, he reported to the Captain who seemed well pleased with the day's work. The lieutenant now pointed out the huge storm clouds forming on the horizon; he estimated it would hit them in two to three hours; he called Petty Officer Adam Luma to the Quarter deck.

"These are my orders you will select five members of the crew to accompany you back to the prize, as she carries six eight pound cannon on her deck you must include two experienced gunners, the privateers crew that are still on board you will place in irons and lock them in the hold, you will then sail her to Boston where we will await you, time is off the essence as a storm is almost upon us"

Adam had no problem with his gunners as he choose able seaman Woods and landsman seaman Williamson their gun crew was the best on the ship, from the other ratings he choose three ordinary seaman Rosser, Pearson, Preston. The six men quickly collected their kit and were rowed over to the Freedom where they joined the other sailors from the Triumph, the privateer's sailors were taken below and placed in irons. By the time this was achieved the wind had got up and was developing into a full gale, the war ship pulled away as she needed to give herself sea room, she turned to face into the storm, the captain fearing that if he ran with the wind he would end up beached on the Mexican shore. Luma was an experienced navigator and knew that his ship having a shallow draught could risk the shallow water off the Mexican coast so he ran with the wind in his sails. As the storm increased he became increasingly worried, he had to reef the sails and furl the jib or risk losing canvas, his crew were used to sailing in huge war ships and half of them were being violently sea sick. The huge waves were now fifty foot high washing over her, the fore and after decks were awash and he feared he may have lost two sailors overboard the gunners were of no use as they were trying to keep the cannon secured to their cleats in the deck, and prevent the gunpowder from getting wet. It required two men at the wheel both of them lashed to prevent them from being washed overboard. The Petty Officer feared that things were getting out of control and they were at risk of foundering he made the decision to seek help from Connolly and his men. He went below to speak to the crew of the privateer he told them he needed help to sail the ship or they would all end up on the bottom of the gulf, his men were all armed and had orders to shoot any of the prisoners who refused an order. For the next twenty four hours both crews worked together to keep the Freedom afloat, she sustained severe damage to her sails and the main mast was leaning at an acute angle. Eventually the storm blew itself out and the sailors managed to take it in turns to get some rest. Adam sought out Connolly who was sleeping in his bunk and informed him it was time to get his men below; he then asked him to accompany Luma to assess what damage the ship had suffered. Both men went on deck and surveyed the damage.

"It looks bad said Connolly, what are your orders?"

"I am to sail the ship and its cargo to Boston where we will rendezvous with the Triumph"

"This ship will never sail to Boston, she won't last a week without major repairs and some new sails, as a deserter from the Kings Navy, only a rope awaits me in Boston, the rest of my men are also deserters, we were headed for the Lafitte Dock in New Orleans which is only a day's sailing away. Should you and your sailors throw in with us we will share the prize money and I feel sure the Gilmore brothers will be very generous to us for bringing the Freedom home."

After listening intently the Petty Officer replied that he would need to consult with his men, he assembled them on the quarter deck and explained in some details the situation they were in. He informed them that the ship was too badly damaged to sail to Boston, he told them of the offer from Connolly and that he could see no alternative. Their own ship the Triumph would have assumed they had sunk in that fierce storm and given them up for lost. He pointed out that America was on the verge of becoming independent from the England and a good living could be had there if you had a few pounds in your pocket. There was much discussion among the men but they all seemed to be in favour of joining the privateers, only Alex had some reservations he needed to get to New York to find his wife and it was a long way from New Orleans. The sailors of the Freedom on hearing this assured him that ships left daily to New York carrying tax free goods for the citizens, he could sign on as a sailor just for a one way journey or pay a small fee and travel as a passenger. When all were in agreement Captain Connolly passed out the rum, then they set too strengthening the mast with timber joists. The sails they had left were enough to make two to three knots and they headed for the Grand Bayou and the little lakes. Two days later they were met on the dock by Charles Lafitte and the Gilmores representative in New Orleans. Connolly told Adam that between privateers and the agents who bought the goods there was complete trust one could not operate without the other. Alex and Graham found digs just behind the docks and got drunk in the local tavern; the following morning they presented themselves at the office to receive their share of the prize money. The two slaves being young strong men fetched a good price in the market, the rest of the cargo was purchased by Lafitte, and the owners of the Freedom chipped in twenty pounds bringing their share of the prize money to £50 each. Alex and Graham wasted no time looking for a berth on an armed schooner heading for New York with a hold loaded with tax free goods.

Chapter Seven Slave Market

Elizabeth was inconsolable for days after Alex was taken, with the help of the older more mature women she began to come to terms with her loss. Two weeks after he was taken the weather deteriorated and the Captain sent all the passengers below then battened down the hatches; she was kept busy helping women whose children were suffering severe bouts of sea sickness. The conditions became intolerable, people were being sick in every nook and cranny the toilet buckets overflowed, the smell was unbearable. The storm lasted for two weeks then the passengers were allowed on deck to wash and clean themselves, as the wind was from the east it drove The John onwards towards the American coast, a week after it abated they had their first sight of land. The passengers lined the rails staring in awe at the houses stretching into the distance; most of them were from villages with no more than twenty cottages. The ship dropped anchor out in the bay and the passengers were ordered to line up on the main deck, the purser set up a table and two chairs for himself and the Captain on the quarter deck.

The passengers were directed up the steps on the starboard side, they arrived before the table singly or in family groups, the purser asked their names and if they had paid their fare in full he handed them their disembarkation tickets. These passengers descended back to the main deck via the steps on the port side where they were helped aboard the lighters waiting to take them to the docks. Those passengers who had paid for their fares by indenturing their services gathered behind the captain's chair, Elizabeth was directed to this small group of six men. When the paid passengers had disembarked several gentlemen came on board, they were known to the captain who called the young men forward the gentlemen being satisfied as to their suitability paid their fare and they left together. Elizabeth was left standing alone; one gentlemen farmer who asked about her was informed that she owed two fares for herself and her man; he had started the journey but was impressed at sea by the English Navy, the owners were insisting she was responsible for his fare too, if it was not paid the owners would stop six pounds from the captains money. The farmer shook his head and walked away leaving Elizabeth alone with the Captain and purser; they looked at her with sympathy then called two sailors forward and ordered them to take her ashore to the slave market. They landed on the East River Docks and walked the short distance to Wall St where she was handed over with a letter from the Captain that she was to be indentured for six years and he required six pounds plus the auctioneer's fee. She was taken into a cell packed tight with black slaves waiting to be sold; they looked at her with surprise and kindness offering her some of their food which she gratefully accepted. The following day she was deprived of her clothing and given a single loose garment open at the front, she was kept to the end of the auction as she was not being sold into slavery. When it was her turn she was led out clutching her garment tight closed, but the auctioneer indicated to his assistant to remove it. She was advertised as a six year indentured domestic servant, most of the buyers were there to buy cotton or tobacco pickers and had no interest in her. One well-dressed man in tricorn hat approached with his wife, he inspected her closely looking at her teeth legs and arms his wife ran her hand over her belly then turning to her husband informed him she was with child with that they walked away. The sale was about to end when a middle aged white man in buckskin jacket called out to the auctioneer that he would take the Irish woman for ten pounds, sold said the auctioneer. Elizabeth was led back to the cell where she recovered her clothes; her new owner was very impressed with her as he recognised good quality garments when he saw them. He introduced himself as Arthur Patton he had arrived in America from Ireland ten years hence; he had a wife and child, his wife was in poor health and she would have to help look after her and the little one. He would find her lodgings for the night and tomorrow they would set off to Philadelphia, Elizabeth was still in shock from her experiences and could only whisper thank you. Her accommodation for the night was in the Travellers Rest where she was given a board and a blanket, she observed the blanket was crawling in lice so she put it to one side, the room was crowded but she found a space in the corner and laid her board on the dirt floor, despite the snoring and farting she had a good night's sleep. Her new master came looking for her in the morning he was driving a wagon fully laden with goods and pulled by two heavy horses.

"What are you called? He asked her.

"Elizabeth Williamson she replied"

"You will be called Lizzy from now on and you will address me as sir or master there is no room on the cart so you will walk behind, stay close as we will be travelling through territory alive with snakes, bears and wolves. The weather is fine so we will sleep under the cart; we could also be attacked by savages so keep alert"

The first day on the Kings Highway they travelled all of fifteen miles, by mid-afternoon Lizzy had discarded her shoes and walked in her bare feet. The trail was wide enough for two carts to pass, later that day the Boston stage coach passed them laden with passengers and luggage, the people on top waved to them but those inside kept the blinds down to protect themselves from the dust. When the light started to fade the master called a halt beside a small stream, while he unharnessed the horses and staked them out on the grass Lizzy got a fire started, when Arthur joined her he was carrying a frying pan a coffee pot and two large pieces of salt pork. They ate their food in silence afterwards Lizzy washed out the utensils in the stream; she then asked Arthur if she could bathe in the stream as it was three months since she had taken a bath. He nodded his head then climbed under the wagon and went to sleep, she washed herself thoroughly in the cold water getting rid of the bugs in her hair, and then she washed her clothes and hung them over the shafts of the cart to dry. She was up and dressed at first light and had a pot of coffee ready by the time he stirred, they ate some strips of dried beef then harnessed the horses Arthur was surprised how efficient she was at handling them, he held up the shafts as she expertly backed the horses between them. Shortly after they started he called to her to come and join him, he was walking along leading one of the horses by the bridle.

"Tell me about yourself Lizzy I see you are wearing a wedding ring, you have the look of a well bred filly, people like you are rare hereabouts, I see you are with child, how long before you pup?"

Before answering him she now felt bold enough to appraise him, he was about the same size as Alex with shoulder length hair going grey, he had the build of a man who had spent a lot of years doing hard work, his face was wrinkled and tanned almost black which made his blue eyed look even bluer. He was dressed in buckskins and had a leather belt around his waist, tucked in the belt was a tomahawk and a flint lock pistol, both looked well used. As the miles passed she told him her life story to date, she said she was looking forward to having Alex's baby and begged him to let her keep the child. He informed her that under the law any child born while she was in bondage was the property of her master to do with as he wished but he would not deprive her of the child while she was wet nursing it. That night while they sat round the fire he told her that he had come from Donegal Ireland with his brother Robert they purchased a small two hundred acre farm, he married his neighbours daughter Margaret Wilson whose father had an adjacent farm, following the marriage the two farms merged and a large timber house was built to accommodate the whole family. They had ten slaves all bought and paid for but he had lost count of the young ones who seemed to be everywhere, they were housed in four log cabins fifty yards from the main house. A year ago almost to the day a band of about fifty rogue Indians attacked the house in the middle of the night, at the time he was up in the hills looking for steers that had wandered. The Indians murdered his brother, father in law and child then scalped them. Margaret and her mother were forced to carry sacks filled with liquor and food that they had plundered before they all set off for the Indian encampment twenty miles distant. That night when they rested several of the young bucks had sport with the women who offered no resistance as they knew their lives would be forfeit. The following day following the combination of abuse she had suffered and the weight she was forced to carry the old woman just lay down and died, the Indians believing she was sleeping jabbed at her with theirs spears when they realised she was dead they just threw the body to the side of the track, after removing the scalp. They forced Margaret to carry on walking with an even bigger load on her back; she knew she would not be able to escape as several of the Indians were mounted on horses they had stolen from the farm; they also had a number of vicious wolf dogs trailing behind them. When they arrived in the Indian village she was made to work late into the night, and when she finally lay down to sleep she had a visit from several young bucks looking to sport themselves. After a month as her health deteriorated the young men left her alone but the squaws still beat her if she didn't carry out her allocated duties, which consisted of fetching water and wood for the fire, she was forced to spend many hours scraping the fat of buffalo hides. They made her dig new latrines every day, and then fill them in as the dogs were feeding on the human excrement. The young men went out hunting every day returning at night with large pieces of buffalo meat, occasionally they had a deer whose hides were prized for moccasins and clothes for the squaws. The men were dressed in a single blanket with a hole in the middle for their head to pass through; they worshipped their chief who ruled them with a strong hand. If he decided the elderly were becoming a drain on the resources of the camp as they had no teeth and were unable to hunt, he ordered the young boys to take them into the woods and dispose of them with their tomahawks. Margaret was brought up to respect the elderly and was appalled at this treatment of the old. When Arthur returned from the hills he found the house a smouldering ruin Coyotes had found the bodies of the dead, and were feeding on them, his first job was to dig a grave and bury them; most of the farm animals had been killed and butchered so he left the carcasses for the wild animals. The slaves had run away at the sight of the Indians, they believed the stories about them skinning and eating black men. They had now returned so Arthur left them to look after the farm, he caught one of the horses wandering in the woods and set off for the Donegal Presbyterian church, on arriving he told the Rev John Kerr what had happened, after listening to

Arthur he advised him to return home and he would arrive with a party of local militia in a couple of days to mount a rescue party. Arthur returned home and began the task of clearing the ruins of his house; he set the slaves to cutting timber for a new cabin. Two days later the Rev. turned up with fifty fully armed mounted men each carrying rations to last a week, Arthur recognised some of his neighbours as Donegal Ireland men, there was Thompson, Clark, Patterson, Dixon, Gray and Elliot. Rev Kerr had made it his business to find out the location of the Indian encampment in the area and after the horses had been watered and fed he led the militia up into the hills where they spent the night. Two scouts were sent ahead to reconnoitre the camp, they located a path in, but it would only accommodate two horses abreast, as the sun was coming up they observed a large party of braves leaving on a hunting trip so they hurried back to the militia. Rev Kerr on hearing this decided not to attack until midday giving the hunting party time to clear the area. At one o'clock after a short prayer the men mounted and rode at full gallop into the middle of the camp, two of the militia men fetched the chief from his tepee with his woman, no one offered any resistance. Rev Kerr had done missionary work with the savages in an attempt to convert them to Christianity; he had picked up some knowledge of their language. Addressing the chief he asked him to bring forward any white captives in the camp, he replied that there was none, whereby the Rev shot his woman point blank in the face the chief's expression did not change. Two of the militia went into the chief's tepee and came out dragging two teen age boys, at this the chief became agitated so the Rev repeated the question, and there was still no response. Tom Gray put a noose over the youngest boys head then set off at full gallop dragging him by the neck around the camp then he pulled up beside the chief and let go the rope. The wails and cries from all the Indians in the camp were pitiful, Gray dismounted collected the rope and put the noose around the eldest son's neck then he remounted. The Rev Kerr repeated the question again, the chief dropped to his knees he called to the squaws to bring the captives forward and Margaret was led out of a tepee supported by two Indian women, Arthur was horrified at the sight of his wife she had been reduced to skin and bones. He asked her if she had seen any other white women in the camp and she replied no, her mother had died on the journey here. The Rev Kerr then informed the chief if he ever had to return to the camp again he would kill all the inhabitants including women and children, you show our families no mercy so in future we will show yours none. Having mounted Margaret on a horse they returned to the farm, the militia stayed for a further two days and helped Arthur to build a sturdy cabin before returning to their homes. Margaret was in a sorry state she could not eat or sleep every time she tried to rest she would wake up screaming, she needed constant care and would allow no one near her but Arthur. After a couple of months he needed to go to New York for seed and various other supplies including guns as he feared the Indians may return looking for revenge, it was while visiting the bank in Wall St that he spotted Lizzy and decided to buy her in the hope she may be able to help with Margaret. After finishing his story he set to making some lead balls for his musket and pistol Lizzy surprised him by helping while he did one size for the musket she made some smaller ones for the pistol. When they had finished he gave her a flintlock pistol also a pouch of gunpowder and a dozen shot together with a belt and a scalping knife.

"Tomorrow we will arrive at the ford, crossing the Delaware, this is the only place you can ford the river and is only available in July-August it is well known to the Tory's and rogue Indians who lie in wait for people like us. Should we be attacked don't hesitate to shoot and save a shot for yourself, you don't want to be taken prisoner by these people"

"Back home from an early age I was trained to defend myself, I am an excellent shot with both musket and pistol" said Elizabeth

They set off for the Delaware at first light Arthur knew he was taking a chance as he could have used the ferry at Trenton but a heavy wagon like his cost a lot of money on the ferry. Half a mile before reaching the ford they pulled into the trees, leaving Lizzy to look after the wagon Arthur went ahead to scout out the trail he approached the crossing with caution, finding no one on either bank he checked the ground on both sides of the river and found it to be firm and dry. When he arrived back he told Lizzy to climb up on the wagon and get a good hold, he perched on the rear of the shaft and started for the crossing, when it came in sight he used the whip on both horses and when they arrived at the ford they were travelling at high speed they crossed the river in a matter of minutes and when well clear of the river they settled to a steady walk on the Kings Highway towards

Lancaster County. This part of the road was regularly patrolled by The Seventh Penn Frontier Rangers; any law breakers captured by them were quickly dispatched usually with a rope on the nearest tree. Having crossed the river they made good time. The country they passed through had been sparsely settled by a mixture of German and Scots Irish farmers, the two different nationalities had little in common but because of the risk of Indian attacks they worked closely together in defence of their lands. Two days later they arrived safely at Arthur's farm in the town land of East Donegal, as they pulled into the yard the black overseer reported to Arthur that everything was in order there had been no sighting of Indians since the raid on their camp and it was believed they had moved further south. One of the female slaves Jenny had been going to the house every day to see to the mistress, she never left the house and needed encouraging to wash and dress, on a few occasions Jenny had to sleep there as the mistress kept waking up in the night screaming. Arthur went immediately to the house after instructing Sam (the overseer) to unload the wagon and show Lizzy where the slaves living quarters where. He entered the house and found Margaret sitting in a chair looking into a fire even though the temperature outside was in the eighties. He took her hand which she immediately snatched away and cowered from him in fear.

"It's Arthur Margaret I'm back to look after you and I promise no one will harm you ever again, I have bought an indentured Irish woman to keep you company she will be up to the house to see you tomorrow"

He got no response from her and went into the kitchen to speak to Jenny.

"Has she been like this all the time I have been gone"

"Yes sir she has not uttered a word since you rescued her from the Indians, she won't eat and cries all the time. She has awful nightmares and wakes up screaming"

"Jenny I will stay with her now you go and find the white slave woman I brought back with me, see she gets some food and somewhere to sleep, tell Sam if anyone lays a hand on her I will hang them"

Jenny knew better than to disobey the master, she showed Lizzy into the cabin she occupied with her man their two children and another childless couple, she found her a bunk along the top wall it had a straw mattress and pillow and one linen blanket which was sufficient at this time of the year. The fire was in the middle of the room with a cast iron pot hanging from a crane. Arthur comforted Margaret in his Arms all through the night and she got some sleep, the following morning he helped her wash and dress then holding her tight led her outside for a walk around the yard. He spotted Lizzy by the water trough washing her face and hands so he led Margaret towards her, when the two women came face to face Lizzy was appalled at the sight of Margaret, her face was pale and drawn and she could not have weighed more than four stone. He invited Lizzy to take his place and suggested she walk his wife over to the corral to look at the horses as she loved them, there was no objection from her and they walked hand in hand over to see the animals. They then made their way back to the house where Margaret once more sat down in her chair by the fire, Jenny had made some bread so Lizzy put some homemade butter on a piece, then attempted without success to get Margaret to eat it. That afternoon she went into the garden and selected a variety of vegetables she placed them in the cast iron pot which was secured by a trammel to a swinging crane over the open fire, she swung the pot out into the room then half-filled it with water. She recovered a smoked leg of pork that was tied to the rafters over the fire, after putting it with the vegetables she lowered the pot to the lowest hole in the trammel and left it to come to the boil. As it began to boil it brought back memories of Dartrey, she remembered the beautiful aroma that permeated the whole house when the cooks were making stews by the time they all sat down to dinner they were famished. She tried once more to get Margaret to talk with her, without success, so she suggested they went to see the horses again, this brought a nod of the head, before leaving Lizzy swung the pot out and raised it to the upper hole in the trammel then left it to simmer. They went to the stables where they spent some time with the horses; they then walked over to the slave quarters, they sat for some time watching the black children playing, she beckoned one little boy whose skin was whiter than the others over, placing her hand on his shoulder she barely audibly muttered.

"This one's Arthurs"

Lizzy thought she had imagined what she heard and said,

"What did you say? But there was no reply and the little boy ran off. It was evening time when they got back to the house, the smell from the stew met them the moment they opened the door, there was a commotion behind them and they turned to find Arthur just in from the fields.

"Mother of God what's cooking?

"I have made a stew in the hope that Margaret might feel hungry and eat some"

"It certainly has made me feel hungry Lizzy, will you lay the table while I get washed?

Lizzie laid the table for her masters and served up the stew as she went to leave Margaret took her hand and indicated she wanted her to sit down beside her, she looked at Arthur, he nodded his head in approval and told her to lay a place for herself, he could hardly believe his eyes at the sight of his wife tucking into the stew with gusto. Before leaving that night Lizzie placed the pot in its highest point on the trammel, it would keep warm and provide dinner for the next three nights. Over the next three months Margaret gained in strength, she and Lizzie became close companions and conversed freely, some days they would hitch up the cart and drive around the farm, but they never went out of sight of the house and they both carried a half-cocked pistol in a waist band.

On Christmas day they attended the Presbyterian meeting house in the east Donegal Chapel, it was a time to mix with other Irish Farmers and have a good chat about crops and the current political situation which was getting more dangerous by the minute. The vast majority of the people felt aggrieved at the taxes that were being imposed on them by a faraway government, and were in favour of a self-governing American state able to elect their own representative's to make laws and issue their own currency. On arriving home the slaves who were mostly Christian had been given the day off and where having their own service in the open, the master wanted to join in with them while the two women went into the house to prepare a slap up turkey dinner. After the meal Arthur asked if he could say a few words, first he said a short prayer of remembrance for those members of the family who were no longer with them, after the prayer he addressed Lizzy,

"Margaret has asked if you could move into the house as it is coming near your time and she wants to be with you when the baby is born"

"Nothing would please me more than to have the mistress beside me when I give birth, this is my first one and I am frightened stiff"

Margaret butted in to the conversation,

"Lizzy! Arthur and I have been preparing the loft; it has a new bed with new clean covers, Arthur has made a cradle for the baby and everything you need to care for the child is there"

"I cannot thank you both enough may God bless you"

It was early morning on the 14th Feb when Lizzy went into labour; mercifully it was a short labour, and just when they were admiring the beautiful baby girl another popped its head out.

"It's twins! Shrieked Margaret and burst into tears, what are you going to call them?

"I had picked two names for my child Fiona Louise, now it will have to be one name for each, first one will be called Fiona and the second one Louise"

"You are blessed Lizzy after the abuse I suffered at the hands of the Indians I will never be able to conceive another child, Arthur is not too concerned as he has a number of children bearing his name among the slaves. When you have recovered he may come to you in the night that is his right with his slaves, you must not reject him as he would be within his right to sell the remainder of your indenture to someone else, you would then be sent away with your new master and the twins would remain here, as they were born while you were his slave that makes them his property.

Privateers Chapter 8

A week had gone without finding a ship when they were contacted by Willy Connolly,

"I know you men have not been successful finding a berth, and the Gilmore brothers would like to talk to us in their office tomorrow, do you want to hear what they have to say it could be to your advantage?

"Why not Graham said, it will not take up much of our time; an extra day will make very little difference"

All three presented themselves at the office the following morning, both Robert and Patrick Gilmore were waiting for them, after sitting them down they were offered a glass of fine Jamaican rum each, which they gladly accepted. Robert Gilmore did the talking.

"Thanks to you men we still have the Freedom, she is in dry dock having a complete refit, another month and she will be sea worthy again, we intend to increase the number of guns she carries to ten six pounders and send her to search the Caribbean and apprehend any pirate ships she should find, with luck her crew may capture some healthy male slaves to sell here in the market. We will also be on the lookout for heavily laden pirate vessels filled with booty stolen from merchantmen"

Now Pat Gilmore chipped in,

"You three could share one quarter of the booty between you, and there could be bonuses for a profitable voyage. You will be carrying, letters of marque issued by THE CONTINENTAL CONGRESS OF AMERICA; ships of most nations will recognise this as your legal right to go about your business"

Alex now pointed out that his first concern was to go looking for his wife that was his first priority.

"Robert informed him that as he had no idea where she was and being a deserter should the British capture him he would be tried and hanged".

He went on to say that they would attempt to locate Elizabeth for him, they knew she arrived last year on The John and the Captain was well known to them. When he returned from the voyage hopefully she would be waiting for him and with his share of the prize money they could buy a substantial farm of land and start a family. Alex asked for time to consider his options, that night in the bar the three men discussed the Gilmores offer both Willie and Graham were in favour but Alex wanted to go in search of Elizabeth. Willie pointed out that it was customary to sell those passengers who could not pay their fare to anybody willing to clear their debt, America was a huge country and she could be anywhere by now. His best bet was to let the Gilmores try to locate her and on return from the Caribbean visit her, the more Alex thought about it the better it sounded.

"O.K what you are saying makes sense; my earnings from this voyage could set me and Elizabeth up for life so you can count me in"

"That does it said Willy I will notify the Gilmores that we have a deal, they will have a lot of instructions to pass on to us, if you are in agreement I will take responsibility for the captains position, but all major decisions will be agreed jointly"

The following day Willy passed on the instructions from the owners he had been given a letter of credit to purchase enough goods for a six month voyage; they were to purchase cannon and ammunition, also a whole list of pistols, knives, and swords, grappling irons would be needed if the opportunity arose to board a pirate vessel. We will pass the word around that we are recruiting sailors for a voyage to the Caribbean and start interviewing in the pub tomorrow night, let us make it known that Captain Connolly will be the master and it should not be too difficult to find sailors as he is well respected. The following day the three men sat at a table in the bar signing up the crew, each man who signed on had to make his mark and it was explained that although Connolly was Captain they were required to obey orders from all three men. Those men who had been selected were informed that The Freedom would set sail on the 2nd Feb weather permitting and they were to report one week early to get everything shipshape including their quarters. When they were alone Willy informed the others that he was well pleased with the crew as most of them were old shipmates who had sailed with him before. Graham who had been carefully studying the men now asked if young Preston could be assigned to him as the powder monkey, Willy agreed and said it was a good choice. The three men visited the ship daily instructing the fitters to amend those things they found not to their liking, they inspected the sails and ropes. As they would be standing three eight hour watches; they agreed to have one comfortable cabin between them. Graham supervised the securing of the gun slides to the deck then the mounting of the guns on the slides, he had a reinforced cabin below decks for storing the powder and shot. Alex secured a number of seven foot long pikes in brackets along the main deck, he then had a secure cupboard built in their cabin which he filled with weapons of all description there would be three keys one each. A week before the sailing date the crew came aboard and started work, three days of grafting and they decided it was safe to take her out for a trial as the weather was perfect. They gently sailed out into The Gulf Of Mexico and when in deep water the captain steered her into position; with a brisk wind from the stern he ordered full sails to be set and she gained her maximum speed of twelve knots. One of the sailors reported that a seam had opened so Willie went below to inspect it; they carried out a temporary repair with some tape and turned back for New Orleans on tying up at the Charles Lafitte dock the foreman of the maintainance crew came aboard for a report. Within the hour the dock workers were back aboard carrying out all the niggling little faults that had been found, she was then moved into dry dock where the seam was sealed with a mixture of linseed oil putty mixed with red lead powder, a little grease was added to keep it subtle, strips of cotton were then forced into the seam before adding the mixture. Prior to sailing Alex and Graham deposited their money in Gilmores bank in return they were given a promissory note for fifty pounds each. On the 04th Feb the owners signed for her and the contractors left wishing the crew a safe journey, after the Captain had made a final inspection he informed the owners he would be leaving at first light. They left on a beautiful morning the temperature was seventy two degrees, and there was a brisk breeze, the crew performed well and the prospects looked good. One day out Graham decided to test the cannon because of the open seam on the trial voyage he had been unable to fire them, he needed to train six extra sailors as in the event of them seeing action he would need extra hands allocated to each gun. After removing the tampion he had the barrel swabbed with a wet sponge, he then loaded the first gun on the port side the charge was rammed down the barrel in a cloth bag, followed by a one pound ball, he estimated the ball would travel 350 yards if the charge was correct, after the chocks were removed from the wheels he charged the flintlock then pulled the lanyard the gun performed perfectly. Over the next week he tested the remaining guns to his satisfaction, he now had enough trained men to man them in action, as he would only be firing either port or starboard at any one time. The three friends ran a tight ship and were not afraid to dish out punishment to those that did not toe the line; two lookouts were located in the top rigging at all times and anyone caught napping got ten lashes of the cat. They were three weeks at sea when the first sail was spotted, they closed on the ship and seeing she was flying an American flag they gave her a wide berth. They spotted an English man o war leaving the port of Trinidad and putting on all sail turned away from her, they were lucky that she had not spotted them. Months went by and they had not located a target after constant training and practice by the boarding parties they were fine-tuned and desperate for action. They were now deep into the hurricane season but so far they had been lucky with the weather, the captain was now reluctant to sail too far from land. He took the Freedom into Port Royal to get some supplies and gather intelligence about Pirate ships that had recently visited the port to pick up slaves and contraband goods. On leaving the port they made for the WINDWARD PASSAGE, this was a busy shipping lane which carried them between Cuba and Haiti, from there they made their way into the Atlantic with the intention of searching the eastern seaboard of America for ships smuggling duty free contraband. Without warning a hurricane was upon them, they reduced sail and turned into the wind, the storm lasted for several hours causing immense damage to The Freedom.

A number of seams opened allowing water to flood in; the sailors formed a chain with buckets and with great difficulty managed to keep her afloat. Other members of the crew were engaged in trying to repair sails, two of the cannons had been wrenched from their moorings and been washed overboard, the powder was saturated with sea water and was useless. During their frantic attempts to carry out repairs a cry went up from the watch

"SAIL HO! ON THE PORT SIDE"

The three men rushed to the port rail and observed an English third class ship of the line bearing down on them; Connolly looked at the other two,

"What do we do we can't outrun her and we cannot fight?

"Let's try to bluff it out, we have no contraband in the hold nor are we carrying any illegal goods we have got Letters of Marque from the Americans"

As the warship came alongside Alex and Graham's heart sank into their boots there in bold letters on her side was the name H.M.S TRIUMPH, the Captain called across to THE FREEDOM

"I am sending a prize crew aboard any man found with arms of any kind will be shot, your captain will return in the boat for interrogation by me"

The Captain called the first Lieutenant to him

"You will take six armed marines and four sailors across to the prize and conduct a thorough search of her; I want to know if any of my previous prize crew are still on board so you will take two of our oldest hands for identification purposes".

The Lieutenant saluted and gathered up his men, each man had a sword and a pistol with ammunition, two of the sailors had been with The Triumph since she first went to sea. When they climbed on board The Freedom they were met by Willy Connolly carrying the signed Letter Of Marque,

"We are a lawful ship carrying on trade between the American ports this is our authority "

The lieutenant told him to take his authority with him and climb on board the boat where he would be rowed across for interrogation by the captain. On climbing on board the warship he made a show of saluting the white ensign then two marines marched him to the Captain's cabin, he was seated behind his table. He stood in front of the table and announced

"I am Captain Willy Connolly operating out of New York with LETTERS OF MARQUE signed by THE CONTINENTAL CONGRESS OF AMERICA; we have the right to trade without hindrance".

Captain John Rosser reached out his hand,

"Show it to me"

He took it and without even glancing at it proceeded to rip it to pieces; he deposited the pieces in the bin.

"America is an English colony and has no right to issues letters of Marque, you sir are a pirate and I must decide what to do with you, I will await the report from the lieutenant searching your ship before making my decision, in the meantime you will be placed in the brig under guard".

Back on the freedom the lieutenant had found nothing incriminating, he wondered why she was so heavily armed and had such a large crew; he lined them up on the main deck for inspection by the two sailors from The Triumph. One of them immediately went up to Graham and put his hand on his shoulder,

 "He was a gunner on our ship, and him too placing his hand on Alex".

Both men were bound to the mast guarded by two marines; they had no hope of escape, they were unarmed and the marines had loaded pistols pointed at their heads. The remainder of the crew were taken below under armed guard, and Alex and Graham were transferred to the Triumph with the remainder of her sailors. Both men were taken before the Captain for questioning; he looked at the men from behind his desk.

"Several months ago you were assigned the task of sailing his Majesty's prize ship the Freedom to Boston and await my arrival, you did not arrive and now I find you in the company of pirates seeking to plunder innocent shipping, can you give me any reason why I don't hang you as deserters"

Alex spoke for them both,

"Sir after you sailed away we were struck by a mighty storm which caused catastrophic damage to the Freedom; she was barely able to float so we had to make for the nearest port. We barely managed to make it and tied up to Charles Laffite's dock in New Orleans where we were made prisoners of the pirates. After spending months in the cells we were offered a berth on the Freedom who having been repaired was about to sail for Cuba to take on a cargo of sugar. We considered this our best opportunity to escape"

"The captain replied I know the part about the storm is true as we, barely survived it, I don't accept the rest of your story, however I can use a couple of experienced gunners for the voyage back to Southampton , I will allow you both to sign on for the voyage, when we land you will be court martialled"

The two men were taken to the purser who issued them with their kit, before reporting to the gun deck, they were issued instructions to load the number ten gun on the starboard side and await instructions. Graham was ordered to align the gun on the Freedoms water line, when he was given the order to fire he hesitated knowing there was twenty men imprisoned in the hold but after a lash of the Coxswains whip he pulled the lanyard. The range was only twenty five yards so a large hole appeared at the water line; those on deck heard the cries of the dying men and those who survived the sinking ship were picked off by the marines, in half an hour all was quiet again and no sign of the Freedom or her crew remained. All crew members were then summoned onto the main deck, to witness the hanging of Captain Connolly he was allowed time to pray before he was hanged from the yardarm, Alex and Graham turned away from the sight of a man they liked and admired struggling and kicking his life away. Captain Rosser gave him a proper sailor's funeral and consigned his body encased in canvas to the deep.

 The voyage back to Southampton was uneventful the two friends kept their heads down and worked hard, the day before they landed in Southampton they were taken down to the brig and placed in irons. After a couple of days locked up they were visited by the first lieutenant who informed them a court martial was being convened to try them for desertion, it may take a few weeks in the meantime they must remain prisoners. Eventually the time came when they were escorted in chains to the Captain's cabin, as they entered they were confronted by an Admiral and two naval captains sitting at a large table, on the table in front of the Admiral at right angle to his body was his dress sword. The first lieutenant spent a couple of minutes reading the charges followed by a lengthy statement about the accused's military career, he then went on to describe the situation regarding the men's appointment as part of the prize crew placed aboard The Freedom with orders to deliver her to Boston. The Admiral then asked Graham why they had not completed the task, and why when she was taken for the second time they were still on board. He explained about the storm and that they were overcome by the privateer's crew and forced to sail to their home port in New Orleans. On arrival they were imprisoned and only managed to gain their freedom, by agreeing to volunteer for a voyage on board the newly repaired Freedom, they agreed in the hope they would get an opportunity to escape. They were assured they were operating with a legal letter of Marque from the Congress of America and would only defend themselves if attacked by pirates. Alex said he had nothing further to add to Graham's account of events, only to say they did not desert their duties willingly. The Admiral now announced that Captain Rosser wanted to say a few words in the defence of the two sailors and he was ushered in.

"Now then Captain what have you got to say?

"Only that I can confirm the truth of some of the story these men have told, on departing The Triumph a huge storm probably the worst I have ever known came down upon us, it was a miracle the prize survived, whenthese men served under me they were hard working and diligent sailors that never gave me any cause for concern, I stand before this court and plead for their lives, they deserve an opportunity to redress the balance and I would willingly take them on board The Triumph for her next voyage. The Admiral and Captains asked that everybody leave the cabin while they considered their verdict. Two hours later they were shown back in Alex noticed that the tip of the sword was now pointing in their direction and knew it boded ill of their chances. All three officers stood while the Admiral read out the verdict.

"Firstly let me thank Captain Rosser for giving evidence on your behalf without it you would both have been hung, standing to my left is Captain Allsebrook he is sailing with a cargo of prisoners to the penal colony of Virginia within the month, it is our unanimous verdict that you join these criminals and travel to the new world, there to serve the rest of your life doing hard work and obeying his Majesty's laws, you will both be tattooed with the letter D on your left upper arm. They were led back to the brig to await transportation to the convict ship, when they were alone Graham told Alex he could not return to America and spend the rest of his life labouring in the tobacco fields.

"England is my homeland and all my family are here, I will look for any opportunity to escape but you must be elsewhere when it happens or you will be blamed and may suffer the noose I want you to have this and he passed his bank promissory note for fifty pounds to Alex.

Alex replied,

"I must return to America to find Elizabeth I know she is waiting for me to come to her, and I will, you are my good friend but from here on in we must go our separate ways"

The following day they were transferred to a prison hulk in Dover where they were branded, and incarcerated deep in the bowels of the ship. They were fed slops twice a day just enough nourishment to keep them alive, fights broke out over spare food left by the dead and dying. Every couple of days they were allowed up on the deck where they shuffled around dragging their chains with them. The two friends barely came in contact with each other but on one occasion while waiting to use the toilet bucket they managed a whispered conversation. Graham told Alex that he had found an old shipmate among the warders who was prepared to help him escape, he had smuggled a file to him and already he was almost through both leg irons, the warder had told him they were to be transferred to the prison ship within the month so he intended going over the side in the next few days. He offered to get the file to Alex, but he declined, wishing his friend good luck in his bid to escape. It was a week later the prisoners were aware of a commotion among the warders, they were taken top side and lined up for counting and searching, and this was done several times before they were sent back down below. Alex lost all track of time then one day they were taken to the heads and hosed down, all bodily hair was removed and they were supplied with new prison clothes. They were loaded into carts and taken to Southampton where they boarded the convict ship Jennifer bound for Virginia, the accommodation was much superior to the hulk, each prisoner had his own bunk similar to those on the immigrant ships, they were allowed on deck each day for exercise and fresh air. Alex discovered from another prisoner that Graham had not been recaptured and no body had been recovered from the sea, he visualised him back home with his family and friends and smiled.

Prior to sailing the captain had the prisoners lined up on the deck, he asked for experienced sailors and tradesmen to stand still the rest were returned to their quarters. Six men remained on the deck when the rest went below; each man was questioned regarding their qualifications when it came to Alex he informed them he had been a gunner on The Triumph. He was asked to volunteer as a gunner on the prison ship for the duration of the voyage in return he would eat and sleep with the crew; he accepted the offer without hesitation. It was nearly two month later when the convict ship Jennifer arrived at Batchelor Bay Albemarle sound West Virginia, a fleet of lighters were waiting to ferry those prisoners who were passed as healthy to the shore. They were marched by the "soul drivers" to the slave market in the harbour there they were packed ten to a cell in the slave prison. They were to be sold at auction the following morning as no funds had been allocated for food to feed them. At seven am the sale started, African slaves were first, good fit young men were sold for about £50 and the women £40, male convicts sold for £10 and women £5, Alex got the best price of the day, as he was not convicted of any violent crime, and he had been sentenced to life, he was bought for £75. The following morning he was collected by his new master, who addressed Alex in a kindly enough way.

"What is your name son?"

"Alexander Williamson"

"I will call you Alex, where do you hail from"

"County Monaghan Ireland"

"Do you belong to that no good drunken, Scots Irish Clan?"

"I do and I am proud of it, how do I address you?

"My name is James Crawford, you will call me Sir or Master, and you are indentured to me for the rest of your life, I will feed and clothe you as long as you do a full day's work in the tobacco fields, we start out for my plantation tomorrow"

Chapter Nine Travelling West

The twins turned out to be a blessing for Elizabeth and the Patton's took them to their hearts, Arthur took his turn at nursing them, he was so obsessed that when the women put one of the baby's down he would immediately pick her up. Despite Margaret's warning he never visited Lizzy at night, but she took no chances and slept with the girl's one on each side. As Margaret had not yet fully recovered she frequently had nightmares and woke up in the night screaming. Lizzy took over most of her arduous duties and they shared the lighter work such as making bread and butter ,the twins turned out to be well behaved, Margaret spent hours just looking at them and at the slightest whimper she would pick them up. The Patton's were good to their slaves they were not overworked and were well fed and clothed; they were grateful for their kind treatment and never attempted to run away. Occasionally they would harbour a runaway slave from a German plantation where they had been cruelly treated,

Arthur would give them food and shelter for a couple of days, and then they had to move on. When the Soul Drivers came chasing them with their hounds Arthur would order them off his land and he threatened to shoot them if they came back. Life was good on the farm but when the twins were ten years of age it became noticeable he was desperately tired when he finished the day's work, he would not discuss his problems with the women. It became noticeable every Sunday after the service the men were spending more and more time in discussion outside the meeting house, these discussions at times ended in heated arguments. One Sunday after service the Rev John Kerr asked the congregation to remain seated as he wished to address them.

"The majority of you sitting before me are tobacco farmers, and for the last couple of years the crops have been so bad you are barely able to make a living, the reasons for this are numerous but hard work is not one of them. You need a ready supply of fertiliser for the soil but this is not available, for the last two years the frost has been the hardest in living memory. I know most of you have been cutting down trees and clearing the roots to give yourselves fresh soil but you are now encroaching on to your neighbours land and you have nowhere left to go. I have heard stories about unlimited free land west of here in the Shenandoah Valley and I propose to gather together a number of my flock to form a wagon train and proceed to the new land. After I have finished speaking if you wish to join me please come forward and give me your names"

When he had finished speaking there was a deathly silence, then everyone started speaking at the same time, they all stopped when they observed Arthur rise and March down the aisle to address the Rev.

"I will come with you John, if I stay I will not be able to feed my family and slaves next year, my lease is due to expire soon and I am certain my rent will increase. I too have been told about the free land in the Carolinas with plenty of water, fertiliser in the form of seaweed can be purchased from the Indians who are friendly. I will need a couple of months to settle my affairs then I will be ready to leave"

Arthur was followed by eight additional farmers, who pledged themselves to the Rev Kerr,

"We believe that God will keep us safe with you leading us Sir, two months from now we will be ready to roll"

On returning to the farm Arthur asked Lizzy to sit down for a talk with him and Margaret, on the table in front of him was a document which he picked up and handed to Lizzy.

" These are your indenture documents you have done your time and are now free, we would like you and the twins to travel west with us but it is up to you I have been told a large contingent of your fellow travellers on the John have settled in the Salem area it is your decision".

"I want to come with you, the slaves are always talking about Salem they say the residents there practice witchcraft and hundreds of them have been hanged for practicing the black arts"

Margaret threw her arms around her; I don't know how I would have managed without you and the twins, now you are no longer an indentured servant we can be sisters and the children will be my nieces".

 "Can they call me Auntie Margaret?

On hearing this twins started jumping up and down calling out

"AUNTIE MARGARET AUNTIE MARGARET"

Then they jumped on her knee and threw their arms around her neck. The following day Arthur had a meeting with the slaves, he broke the sad news that he would have to sell them as he needed the money to buy a Conestoga wagon and the horses to pull it. As he was entering the unknown he would have to go prepared carrying with him seeds and goods to live on for at least two months. He gave them his word he would not separate immediate families, and only sell them to farmers with a good reputation for caring for their slaves. They would remain with him until departure time as he would need them to prepare the wagon, and drive the livestock to the market; he was taking two milk cows with him as the twins would need milk. Both women set too collecting everything they would need on the journey, a selection of good quality walking boots, clothes for all eventualities, pots and pans and all cooking and eating utensils including a crane and trammel for cooking over an open fire. The men travelled in a group to Pittsburgh to buy their wagons and horses, The Rev felt they would have more buying power if they went together to the horse traders and wagon makers. After agreeing a price the dealers undertook to deliver a wagon and horses to each individual farmer within six weeks. Arthur found a German farmer, who had a good reputation for dealing fairly with his slaves. He agreed a price with the farmer to take over the remainder of the leases on his abandoned farm, it would give him an additional eight hundred acres, this would allow him to rotate his crops and maintain good healthy soil but he was in need of more slaves. The following day they were summoned to a meeting with the Rev in the Presbyterian Church, he informed them that there were a number of issues to be agreed upon,

1 they would need someone to look after the medical needs of the trekkers,

2 They would need the services of a vet to deal with sick animals,

3 They would need the services of a mechanic to repair broken wagons.

4 they must agree jointly to help any person in the wagon train unable to continue because of illness or injury.

Now they had identified the key people that would be required on the journey the question was where to find them and could they afford to pay them, Archibald Armstrong raised his hand and volunteered to be the mechanic he was good at repairing wagons and would require no payment. John Craig then raised his hand and volunteered to look after both sick people and sick animals, he had a reputation as a healer and he offered his services for free, George Gibson volunteered his services as farrier he had two grown sons who were both capable of shooing horses and making hoops for the wagon wheels. They agreed that each wagon would carry some spare parts, as the wagons were all the same make it limited the number of spare parts that would be required. So far the meeting was progressing well then the Rev dropped his bombshell, he proposed that they follow the example of God and not travel on the seventh day this should be a day of rest. The meeting erupted in a storm of protest only the Rev and elder Arthur Patterson were in agreement, the rest felt they needed to push on, they had over eight hundred miles to travel at a rate of ten to fifteen miles a day, and the journey would take at least two months. A compromise was finally reached when they all agreed to make camp early on a Sunday and attend services, followed by some recreational singing and dancing they were fortunate to have some good musicians among the travellers. The meeting broke up and the farmers returned home, Arthur had purchased several bags of seed and a large tub of Bear grease for the hubs on the wagon. The farmer who was taking the lease on Arthur's farm came to see him, his son who was due to wed would like to buy the farmhouse and outbuildings he offered a generous price and it meant the slaves could remain in their huts. The wagon arrived in time and every inch was inspected by both Arthur and the twins who never left his side, it was twenty two foot long and ten foot to the top of its stout canvas cover, it came complete with tools and harness, the horses were already in the corral. They would need eight horses, six to pull the wagon with two tied to the tailgate their job would be to replace any horse showing signs of tiredness and would also help to pull the wagon up steep hills, being tied on the back they would help slow it on a steep downhill. All three grownups had to learn to harness the horses to the wagon and take their turn to drive the team; they became proficient but knew they had rivers and mountains to cross which would test them to the utmost of their ability. They decided to take the farm cart and two lighter horses to transport the items they would need daily for cooking, non-perishable food, clothing, and ablutions the twins would ride on this cart with their mother while Arthur and Margaret would ride on the wagon. They had a large fifty gallon water barrel secured with a bracket to the side of the wagon; this would need filling up at regular intervals as it had to supply drinking water for ten horses and five people, they had a smaller barrel also secured filled with bear grease. The wagon train was scheduled to assemble at the church on the twenty second of September; The Patton party had spent the previous two ways loading the wagon with a large supply of baled hay and oats and all their farm implements, they took all the house hold items they could load Arthur estimated he had a load of seven or eight tons on the wagon. Behind the cart were tied, two milk cows. The day before they were due to assemble they set out for the meeting spot, and took their place in the line, the Rev Kerr went along the line of wagons inspecting everything, all the families had prepared themselves and their equipment to the best of their ability. That evening they held a service and were introduced to Joe a Christian Cherokee Indian who was to help guide them along the Great Wagon Road better known to the Cherokees as the Warriors Path, generations of Indians followed the buffalo down this path. The following morning at first light the noise was deafening as the horses were harnessed into the wagons; men were shouting women were crying, a number of the men showed their inefficiency, but those who had prepared properly went to their aid and eventuality they started off, with the Rev leading. Joe strode out in front with his dog running beside him; they had to stop on a number of occasions for harness to be adjusted, by the time they camped for the night they had only travelled five miles. For the first time since they were born the twins had other children to play with and they loved it, Lizzy never saw them only when they wanted food. The road was quite good, at this stage it was regularly travelled by people going between Lancaster and Philadelphia, the road was dotted with log cabins, and small settlements had grown up at every cross roads. They were able to buy fresh food at these settlements but found it expensive, some of the men visited the saloons which were numerous and well stocked with all sorts of alcohol. On making camp at night everybody including the children had to set about filling water troughs for the animals to drink, they then had to distribute the hay among their animals. While the others attended to the chores Lizzy lit a fire and prepared a cooked meal after they had eaten they attended prayers led by Rev Kerr, they then dispersed to their beds. They arrived at Wrights ferry to find they would have to wait four days to cross, they got in line and used the time to carry out a number of repairs to their vehicles, and they also used the time to replenish the animal fodder and drinking water. Having crossed the ferry they travelled North West to the Susquehanna River once again they were delayed at the Harris ferry, by this time the populated areas were getting thin on the ground. The great wagon road was getting narrower each day, they were travelling through dense forest alive with wild animals hardly a day went past without a sight of a bear and the perimeter of the camp had to be patrolled at night with men and dogs. They passed through York then turned southwest through Maryland into Virginia, after passing Winchester they entered the Shenandoah Valley which ran between the Blue Ridge and Alleghany mountains. They encountered numerous steep hills at the worst they had to part unload the wagon and carry their goods up on their back, on the downslopes to prevent the wagons running away they secured heavy trees to wagon slowing down its decent. They caught Ingles ferry at Big Lick (Roanoke) this time they were only delayed two days, it gave them time to replenish their supplies fill the water barrel and most importantly grease the hubs of the wagon and cart. The Rev Kerr decided to make a stop at Fort Chiswell they now had a choice to make, they could either continue south into North Carolina or Southwest into Tennessee. After a two day well-earned rest in the fort they had a meeting to discuss their route, both had their advantages and disadvantages. Heated arguments occurred at the meeting they agreed that sticking together was best but four wagons were determined to take the wilderness road through the Cumberland Gap into Tennessee while the rest wanted to continue south through Carolina. They argued late into the night and finally decided to divide into two groups Elder Arthur Patterson would lead Joe Elliot, Joseph Murray, and Willy Mc Carthy into Tennessee where they would look for good farmland. The remainder including the guide Joe would remain with the Rev travelling south they would leave on the morrow for Salisbury and on into North Carolina the second party needed to find a guide so they would remain in the fort for a couple more days. The guide Jo, led Rev Kerr and the six remaining wagons set out on the Great Valley Road; the road had narrowed considerably and was nothing but an animal path through thick forests. They were making very little progress and were forced to send two men ahead with axes and guns; they cleared the fallen trees and branches from the road they also hunted and shot the plentiful game, leaving a carcass or two at the nights camping spot. It took several weeks to reach the Appalachian Mountains and five weeks of back breaking effort to cross them, the strong had to help the weak who at times felt they could not go on. They were now in Mecklenburg County and in frequent contact with bands of Indians mainly Cherokee most were friendly but others demanded horses or cattle for allowing them to proceed, Joe was constantly negotiating with his fellow tribesmen to allow them free passage. With the influx of white men and women the Indians were being driven further and further south, away from their traditional hunting grounds, they showed signs of severe hardship a number of them were dressed in just a single woollen blanket woven by their women. Jo managed to get the help of several braves to help negotiate a particular hilly part of the trail these men carried load after load on their backs up the steepest inclines and helped slow the wagons down on the steep descent, in return they received food and clothing. Each evening they returned to their own camp with meat and clothing for their families. Then one day they did not appear, the Rev, gave Jo permission to go to the camp and look for them. On returning he asked if John Craig could visit the camp as the people appeared to be suffering from a severe form of sickness. The following day on reaching a clearing by a small stream the wagons formed a circle and John Craig packed his medicines and set off with Jo for the Indian village. The remainder set too repairing their wagons, George Gibson and his two sons replaced the worn and broken shoes on the horses. The women used the time to wash the clothes in the creek then repair any item that had holes in them, the water barrels were filled to capacity. John Dixon killed and butchered a steer, the meat was salted and divided among the wagons the two outriders returned and spent their time hunting deer whose skins were needed for new outer clothing, the undergarments woven by the women before leaving were still in plentiful supply. John Craig and Jo returned a week later, after speaking to the Rev outside the camp a meeting was held with all the families and they were told what John had found at the Indian encampment, on arrival he had observed dead bodies scattered about on the ground some were being eaten by wolves and dogs, they searched the camp for signs of life but found none. One young women in the throes of death informed Jo that the people not infected by the disease had deserted the camp leaving the sick to die; a shiver went through John as he recognised the symptoms as Small Pox, a disease he had first encountered in Philadelphia. He forbade Jo to touch any of the bodies and they both made a hasty retreat. On arriving at the outskirts of their camp he called for the Rev but refused to enter the camp. On seeing the Rev approach John called to him to come no closer.

"Why what is the matter? He called out,

"It was SMALL POX the whole of the Indian village was wiped out, you must not come near us as we may be contaminated".

"What do you want me to do?

"You will deliver new clothes to a spot downstream; we will go looking for them in one hour's time",

"Leave it to me" replied the Rev returning back to the camp.

One hour later the two men found the clothes, they removed the garments they were wearing and sprinkled them with their gun powder; using their flint locks they set fire to them, they then entered the creek and washed their bodies thoroughly before returning to the bank and dressing in their new clothes. They then returned to the camp and told the remainder of their experiences at the Indian encampment. It was agreed they would set off at first light the following morning John warned the rest that for some time they had received assistance from the young men from that village and that they must be on their guard for any signs of disease. He told them that the first signs are flu like with head and muscle ache, should anyone notice these symptoms they should send for him immediately. Without the help of the young Indian men the journey got tougher, and they could only manage five miles a day. The outriders returned one day to inform them of a small settlement nearby called Charlotte; as they approached they were stopped at the outskirts and informed Small Pox was rife in the village, they had it contained but no strangers were being allowed to enter. It was two weeks after the episode at the Indian village when Louise complained to her mother about feeling ill, she had a high temperature with projectile vomiting. John Craig was sent for to examine her, he said it was early days to diagnose THE SPECKLED MONSTER but he would examine her every day. A few days later he spotted the red spots around her mouth and a shiver went through him, a halt was called and he informed the rest that Small Pox was among them. It was agreed that Arthur and his family should be isolated from the rest, Lizzy wanted Fiona to stay with their friend Sam Gray he was in agreement but the others objected, Fiona settled the argument by saying she was not leaving her sister while she was alive. The wagon train came to a small clearing and Arthur pulled his wagon out of line, the others made sure he had a sufficient Quantity of food and water then proceeded on their journey. It was late afternoon the following day when they observed the return of two of the wagons it was John Dixon and Sam Gray John's wife and Sam's youngest Daughter were smitten by the disease. The next day the three remaining wagons returned following a meeting they had agreed sticking together was the best option, they had all been in contact with someone suffering from the illness so it would be best to help each other beat the disease. John Craig now took charge he insisted the bedding and clothing of those contaminated be burned; those suffering from high fever should have their forehead cooled with a wet cloth. Next to go down was George Gibson's youngest son; those who were nursing the sick were stretched to the limit as the patients needed twenty four hour a day care. Louise had now developed sores which erupted on the skin; and developed a rash on her body; she was in agony and cried all the time Fiona never left her side even sleeping by the side of the bed. She had been at deaths door for nearly three weeks when John Craig noticed the sores were beginning to scab over.

Most of the scabs were on her back and buttocks, he also noticed her fever was abating so he took Lizzy to one side and informed her Louise would survive with only a few scars where the scabs had fallen off. They had been in the clearing for most of a month when young Gibson departed this world, followed by Rebecca Gray, John Dixons wife survived but she would be blind for the rest of her life. When the disease seemed to have retreated a meeting was called by John Craig, he declared the epidemic over and announced that those who had survived would be immune in the future. He suggested the survivors exchange a small quantity of blood with those who were still susceptible to the disease, he had seen this done in Philadelphia by applying a small cut to the arms and holding the cuts together this transferred some immune blood to the person at risk. The Rev Kerr after Sunday service recommended this action to his flock who without exception proceeded to carry it out. The wagon train now continued onward towards Charlotte which was now disease free; the residents still checked new travellers for any sign of disease before allowing them to stop in the village.

CHAPTER 10 UNREST

Crawford collected Alex the following morning in a cart drawn by two strong shire horses; the road was just a track with two wheel ruts, it ran due east and despite the poor road they were able to make twenty miles a day. Alex had been travelling for four days before he dared ask his new master what their destination was, at first he ignored him but as Alex persisted he finally informed him that he had a plantation of one hundred acres near Johnsonville and he expected they would arrive in the next two to three days. He now began to loosen up a bit and asked Alex what crops he was familiar with on being told he laughed, that sort of farming is for old women, on my farm we grow cotton and corn. I own twenty slaves and their families, what I need now is an overseer to allow me more time to socialise and participate in politics and sport, I enjoy bear baiting ,cock fighting and horse racing. I have one Negro who looks after my cockerels and two fine blood stallions, one of which has just won the Carolinas challenge cup with my son on his back. You will be given your own hut and your job will be to ensure the slaves do a good days work, most of them are a lazy lot so you will be required to lay on with the whip on a regular basis. On the sixth day they pulled into the small town of Sanford where Crawford loaded up the wagon with supplies, he spent the night in the small hotel while Alex slept in the hay loft above the stables guarding the supplies, the following morning they set off on the final lap of their journey. By mid-afternoon Crawford's plantation was in sight but it took another four hours to arrive at a large dwelling house nestling among a small pine forest, fifty yards from the house was a shallow lazy river flowing with sparkling clean water. They pulled into a large yard with a row of huts laid out in a semi-circle the cart stopped next to a large timber barn. Two black slaves arrived immediately and began unloading the contents and carrying them inside, Crawford jumped down and recovered a box of goods before heading for the house. Alex unharnessed the horses, then after hanging the harness up he led the horses to the corral where there was an ample supply of hay and oats. A handsome young black approached him,

"Are you the new overseer he asked?"

"I am he replied what are you called?"

"My name is Aaron Crawford and I am fifteen years of age, I am the best jockey in all the Carolinas"

"Pleased to meet you Aaron can you show me where my cabin is and where I might get something to eat?"

"If you follow me I will show you"

He led Alex across the yard to a small cabin which stood alone; it was situated between the black slave huts and the master's house. Inside was a single bunk bed and a small fire place with a swinging crane and a small cooking pot hanging on a chain, there were additional cooking utensils at the side of the fireplace. One square aperture in the front wall and one in the rear allowed light in and smoke out. A rap came on the door and Aaron stood there.

"I told my mammy you were hungry and she has prepared you some food, if you will follow me and with that he set off across the yard followed by Alex".

The cabin he entered was neat and clean, with a large table which he was told to sit at, a bowl of stew was laid before him with a large ear of corn. In the dark interior he could barely make out Aarons mammy but when she finally came into view he was surprised to note she was more white than black, a handsome woman slightly overweight as were most of the female slaves. After thanking her for the food he returned to his cabin where he slept soundly till daylight. He had washed and shaved in the morning by the time Crawford arrived.

"You can go and get some breakfast from Martha then meet me at the stables" he was told.

Thirty minutes later he arrived at the stables where he was invited to choose a saddle horse for himself, he took some time selecting a strong quiet mare; he knew that in this part of the world he may have to rely on his horse to save him from the Indians and Tories(bandits) in the surrounding hills.

"Good choice said the master approvingly; if you follow me I will show you around the estate"

He spent the next four hours riding around showing Alex the different features, by far the largest crop was cotton and he was given a lesson on planting and harvesting, as it was now showing white as far as the eye could see he was informed they would start harvesting the following week. It would be Alex's job to supervise the black slaves and be sure that fit healthy men gathered two hundred and fifty pounds a day. The crop gathered by the women and children would be left to his discretion but he must ensure they produced to their maximum ability. Ten acres of cleared land was covered in rotting sea weed, Crawford intended to plant this area with winter corn, some of which he would sell, the rest would be ground and used for animal and human feedstuff. As they got closer to the house he pointed to several acres that were being used for growing potatoes, and vegetables of all kinds, the weather in this area was so mild these crops could be planted and harvested at any time of the year. He informed Alex fertiliser was cheap and in plentiful supply, the local Indian tribes dragged large bundles of sea weed of the beaches behind draught horses and were usually paid in whiskey and cotton, which the women spun into rough cloth to wear under their animal skin outer clothes. After they returned the horses to the stables Alex was shown to the store house where he selected a rabbit and some vegetables for a stew, he was given a key to the door and informed that only he and Martha had access. The following day Aaron introduced him to the remaining black slaves most of them acknowledged him but refused to give him eye contact, without exception they looked at the bullwhip he carried in his right hand. That evening he was invited up to the house to meet the rest of the Crawford family, James Crawford was a member of the lower house of the North Carolina legislature and aspired to live the life of an aristocrat. His wife Agnes was also of Scots descent a handsome woman slightly overweight and dressed in the latest European fashion, he had two daughters Bridgid and Anne aged fifteen and seventeen both unmarried which was unusual for North Carolina where women were in short supply. A young adult man stood in the background and when introduced to Alex as Donald he avoided looking him in the eye or offering any signs of recognition. After the introductions the young people left the adults in the kitchen and retired to the parlour. When they were alone Agnes asked Alex about his background, and he gave her details of his life story to date.

"So you are married then, but you don't know where your wife is, how do we know you will not run away at the first opportunity to go looking for her".

Alex showed her the large D tattooed on his arm.

This has marked me as a naval deserter Ma'am should the loyalists or the British army capture me I will be hanged on the nearest tree, better for me to stay here and try to earn my freedom by loyalty to the master and working hard.

"Very commendable Alex, as your master is a member of the lower House of Representatives and spends much of his time attending to political matters we will be relying on you to protect the family and see to the day to day running of the estate, we don't entirely trust the slaves".

"I will do my best Ma'am, so far I have found no reason to doubt the trustworthiness of the blacks and I intend to treat them fairly and show them respect".

"That's fine but don't be too soft with them" said Agnes"

The following week the picking of the cotton began, everybody with the exception of the family was expected to participate, the temperature was eighty degrees in the shade, but there was no shade, the air was thick with Mosquitoes and there were snakes everywhere. Corn bread and water was fed to the workers at midday, twenty minutes was all they were allowed to eat and answer the call of nature. Despite the heat most of the slaves met their quotas, occasionally a halt would be called in one area as a rattle snake had been spotted, the pickers were accompanied by several dogs who were expert at tracking and killing snakes. The farm carts carried the cotton back to the big barn where they were baled by a firm of carters who were employed to transport the bales to the coast; there they were loaded on ships for transporting to several European ports. The destination depended on who was paying the best price at that time. When the last bale left the estate the Crawford's threw a party for the slaves, a number of pigs and hens were killed, together with the rabbits and vegetables from the store house they produced a fine feast. The family spent an hour helping to serve up the food then left to return to the big house for their private celebrations. After they departed a large quantity of corn whisky was produced, music and dancing began and went on into the early morning.

The next stage of the cotton production was cutting the stalks, followed by ploughing the ground; it was then covering with fertiliser. Come May the seeds would be planted in shallow trenches then covered with soil, three months later the blossoms would appear, they would fall off to be replaced by cotton bolls, they would then split revealing the pure white cotton. As the next few years past Alex became an expert at growing cotton and the Crawford's were happy to leave the running of the estate to him. The master spent less and less time at home as the situation between America and England deteriorated, both his daughters were married and moved away by seventeen seventy six. James had returned to celebrate the New Year with his wife. He sent a message to Alex to come up to the house for a meeting, this time he was ushered into the drawing room Mr and Mrs Crawford were both seated waiting for him.

"I know I have been absent a lot of the time Alex and have relied on you to manage the estate; you have done a good job and my wife and I are deeply grateful, we have tried to treat you kindly and I hope you appreciate that. North Carolina is on the verge of mutiny, and every adult male over sixteen is required to join the militia. Our son Donald has been summoned to join the Johnsonville militia by the end of January; there lies our problem if he were to go he would need to take his mother, to look after him. Under the law we can appoint a substitute to act in his place; this cannot be me as I am needed in the state capital, it is my opinion we will be the first state to declare independence".

Mrs Crawford had moved over in front of Alex taking his one hand in both of hers she knelt down.

"Please help us Alex he may be a tall strong adult aged twenty five but he has the mind of a ten year old child"

All the staff had a great love of Donald he would frequently wander around the yard playing with the children and patting the animals, he would obey commands from any adult even the slaves, all attempts to get him to ride a horse or drive the cart failed, he had very little co-ordination failing even to catch a ball when the children threw it to him.

"You cannot be forced to join as you are not an American but you can volunteer to be a substitute for an American citizen, if you do this for us we will consider your position here on the plantation" said James.

"I will do it said Alex but I will need my own horse and musket, you must supply me with ball and powder also food"

As the men now began to talk business Agnes arose to her feet after thanking Alex she left the room, James then went to the sideboard got two glasses and filled them with good quality French brandy. He offered the brandy to Alex then produced a box of fine Cuban cigars, when they were settled James took his seat again.

"We Americans have had enough of English taxes they refuse us permission to print our own money and insist that we board their soldiers in our homes with no recompense, the royal Governor has done a bunk and taken up residence on board a British war ship anchored at Wilmington, he is currently attempting to raise an army of English regulars together with Scots settlers who are loyal to the King. They are intending to march and join him at Wilmington but we intend to block their way at Cross Creek, this will force them to head for the bridge at Moore's Creek where we will be waiting. You must travel post haste to join the Johnsonville militia and report to Col Bryan and his brothers at New Bern I suggest you start at first light, young Aaron will take over your duties here".

That evening Alex said his goodbyes to the slaves, who were sad to see him go, he cleaned his musket and bayonet then packed his powder in a waterproof bag ready for the journey. The following morning he was presented with a bag of food and James Crawford pressed two gold coins into his hand, then he departed at a steady trot. Most of the early part of his journey was through thickly wooded forest, he was on the lookout for any Cherokee Indians as they had sided with the royalists who were paying them well for every American scalp they handed in to the fort. The following day Alex approached Fayetteville and found more of the militia heading the same way, they received intelligence that the combined British forces of regular's militia and Cherokee were mustering in Brunswick before marching to Wilmington. The patriots in Alex's group received orders to report to Col Lillington at Moore's Creek Bridge so they turned south and on reaching the creek were placed in defensive positions; the patriots were in a good mood and looking forward to the fight with the royalist's. That night Alex was ordered to do guard duty he patrolled both sides of the creek crossing back and forth across the bridge, as he patrolled behind the line he came across a familiar sight, a pair of cannon, he enquired from the Captain of the Guard who was responsible for using them and why they were not covered to protect them from the weather. He replied that as no one knew how to fire them, they were just there as ornaments, he got very excited when Alex told him he was a trained naval gunner. They went together to examine the cannon one was a six pounder iron cannon in a filthy condition, there was ammunition side boxes on each side and on inspection they were found to contain a large quantity of cannon balls, the other box contained powder all bagged up and ready for use they checked a small amount of powder from several bags and found it to be dry and serviceable. When daylight appeared the captain took Alex to

Colonel Lillington's tent, without any preamble he blurted out,

"Col I have found a real gunner, he served as a gunner with the Royal Navy for a couple of years"

"This is a miracle; it's the last place I would expect to find a cannoneer, do you think you could get those antiques to work"

"Give me six men and I will have those guns ready for action this time tomorrow"

"Oh my god wont the British be surprised, turning to the Captain, give him anything he needs give him six of our very best men, now away with you and get cracking"

Alex returned to the guns for a further inspection the six, pounder was mounted on a limber this is how it would be fired but one of the wheels was damaged with broken spokes.

"We need a replacement wheel or that one repaired by lunch time today; we also need a four foot high tree stump to mount the other one on"

"Leave it to me replied the Captain"

The second cannon was a half-pound swivel gun often called a bow chaser, beside it was a canvas covered ammunition trailer full of powder and shot, the men were set to cleaning both cannon, inside and out. By lunch time the tree stump and repaired wheel were returned, two foot of the tree stump were buried in the ground the soil was packed tightly around it and the surface was made smooth. The swivel gun was then placed on top and the base was secured by wooden pegs into the stump. The gun could now be sighted by a kneeling man and swivelled through one hundred and eighty degrees without difficulty. Alex now began intensive training with his gunners he allocated one the job of ramming the shot, another was responsible for the powder, he would sight and fire the cannon then while it was being reloaded he would fire the swivel gun late in the afternoon both guns were ready for action and they were satisfactorily tested with a blank charge with Col Lillington looking on with a smile on his face.

Daybreak Feb 27 1776 the loyalist arrived at the bridge as some of the planks had been removed they were forced to cross by the girders, the patriots opened fire with both musket and cannon, the loyalists were taken completely by surprise as they were not expecting to encounter cannon shot. The battle only lasted thirty minutes, the loyalists having sustained heavy casualties broke and ran with the patriots in hot pursuit. Alex stayed with the cannon and had them both cleaned in readiness for a counter attack but none came. Word of the victory reached the state legislature and soon after North Carolina declared independence. Within a week the militiamen started to drift back to their farms as it was time to prepare the ground for cotton planting. Colonel Lillington sent for Alex, shaking him by the hand he congratulated him commenting that the cannon had made a difficult job easy; he also wished to be remembered to James Crawford and Agnes. The following morning he mounted his horse and headed back to the estate where he was warmly welcomed by the workers. Agnes Crawford and her son Donald invited him to have Sunday lunch, they were anxious for information on every tiny detail of the battle and Alex obliged them sparing none of the gory details Donald clapped his hands together and giggled with delight when he heard of the suffering of the loyalists. The following day he rode around the fields, he could find no fault with Aaron's preparation for the planting of the cotton seed in April or May. Later in the week James Crawford came home and sent for Alex without delay, this time he was shown straight into the drawing room where after taking a seat he was presented with a glass of brandy and a Cuban cigar.

"I have a document to show you, with that he went to his desk and retrieved an official looking paper with a wax seal and several signatures. Alex this is your freedom but there are some conditions attached, Col Lillington attended our meeting to give his report on the battle at Moore's Creek he heaped praise on your part in the victory. We had no idea you were such a brilliant gunner and we are desperately in need of people with your skills. We want you to travel to Fort Sullivan and take up a position as Captain of the South Carolina artillery, the fort is in the process of being built and we are expecting an attack by the British navy at any time. There are more than thirty cannon of various sizes but what we are desperately in need are trained gunners. If the fort falls it will be the end of Charleston, you will be required to sign regular papers for the duration, and in return you will receive the rank and pay of a Captain, I will buy your uniform he said with a smile".

"I will do it" said Alex without hesitation and they shook hands, Crawford gave him his papers and he was a free man.

Chapter 11 War

The Rev Kerr noticed a number of townspeople enter their camp and joined in the services, on finishing he was approached by two men who introduced themselves as representing the Charlotte Committee of Safety. They were responsible for the conduct of the residents of the town, who they said were badly in need of spiritual guidance and educating in the mysteries of the bible. The Rev pointed out that he was only passing through on his way further west where he hoped to set up a farming community with the members of the wagon train. James Young a member committee elected himself as spokesman and addressed the Rev,

"We have a stout cabin next to a creek which was abandoned by the Stewart family when small pox first struck the community, in addition there is ten acres of good arable land we own the deeds to this land and would sign it over to you, if you agree to stay and be our vicar. The Population is currently two hundred plus, most of whom are Presbyterians, we will come together under your guidance to build a new meeting house and school and allocate you a stipend of eighty dollars a month"

"That is very generous of you James but the ascendant Church in Mecklenburg County is the Church of England, under their rules I am unable to legally carry out any christenings, marriages or burials".

"The citizens of Charlotte do not recognise the laws of England, currently we are boycotting all her goods and in the near future we will be declaring our independence"

"I will need to discuss what you have said with my family and friends, can you give me a week to make a decision"

"That will be fine" replied James Young.

John Kerr spent most of the evening discussing the offer he had received from the citizens. His family declared their opposition to further travel, rumour was rife that war with the British was imminent and the Indians had taken their side, the next stage to Columbia was swarming with Indian savages who preyed on wagons passing down the trail. The Kerr family were unanimous that they should settle in Charlotte and make it their home. The following day he gathered the remaining families together and told them of his decision to remain in Charlotte and preach to the community in and around the small town. The following day he made his decision known to the committee. Archibald Armstrong and John Craig were in favour of carrying on, but the remainder wished to think about it some more. The following day they enquired about the availability of free land in Mecklenburg County, they soon found that the King George had granted rights to most of the land to Lord Selwyn who would let it on lease at about four English pounds an acre, the rent to be reviewed annually. As these Scots Irish had left Ireland to avoid the robbing English landlords, they were not going to fall for their thieving ways again, here in the new world. Arthur Patton decided to stay and to include Eliza and the twins in his decision , Margaret and Lizzy were all for it, Lizzy wanted the twins to go to school and grow up as educated young women able to read and write, she also felt if she stayed put Alex would have a much easier job of finding her. As a well-educated woman she could apply for the job of teacher when the new school was built. Arthur then broke the news to them that he intended to join the patriot army for the duration of the war which was coming in the near future. Arthur made his decision known to the remaining families who had all decided to carry on, only he and the Rev Kerr would be remaining in Charlotte with their families. By the end of the week the wagon train pulled out on the arduous road to Greenville, they made their sad farewells to those remaining, they had been informed that south of Augusta there was a virtually unlimited supply of good free farming land with an abundance of water an wild animals.

Arthur reported to Captain Polk of the Mecklenburgh County militia within the week, he signed up with them for the duration of the war, he was given a homemade pike and an axe, guns were only available to soldiers of the continental army, he began military training and his excellent shooting and aggressive abilities soon brought him to the attention of the Captain who promoted him to Lieutenant and gave him his own platoon and horse. Meanwhile the schoolhouse together with a comfortable two bedroomed cabin had been built by the citizens and Liza was appointed as the teacher. On opening the school on the first day she was swamped by about forty pupils of all ages, this brought in enough income to employ Margaret as her assistant. Now Charlotte had a Church and a school it began to expand and prosper, Arthur managed to visit Margaret on occasions, the residents were patriotic to the core and he felt safe in his new home town. They disposed of all their goods and horses after parking the wagon up behind the schoolhouse. The twins who are now eleven helped to teach the younger children and attend senior classes to expand their own knowledge. Early in February Captain Polk mustered his men on the parade ground he informed them that he had been ordered west to join a number of other patriot units who were attempting to prevent a large well-armed body of loyalist from joining Forces with a number of English regiments at Wilmington. It took two weeks to get men and supplies together; some of the men had livestock and crops to attend to and the Captain managed to borrow muskets, ball and powder for the men who were travelling with him. The fifty mounted men and supply wagons set of through heavily forested country, travel was slow the Captain had been ordered to rendezvous with Colonel Richard Caswell at the bridge over Moore's Creek no time limit had been set. Three days into the journey they began to meet up with North Carolina minute men and militia, they told the story of the great battle and how the patriots had routed the British killing hundreds and taking large numbers of prisoners, it was later when the truth emerged that some of this story was found to be an exaggeration but it did not detract from the importance of the victory. A despatch rider arrived with orders for Captain Polk to travel south east towards Martinborough and intercept any loyalists he may find fleeing the battle at Moore's Creek. The patriots found the going tough they headed south towards the known Tory stronghold of Elizabethtown which they bypassed, they avoided any villages in order to keep their presence secret. Turning west towards Martinborough they encountered a small band of mounted loyalists, just outside the town, the fifty patriots charged with their pikes but the loyalists fled towards the town, the patriots hard on their heels, when the town came into sight the Captain called off the chase and turned north in the direction of Charlotte. He left six men as a rear guard in case the loyalists came after them but as they had been careful not to leave a trail no pursuit developed. When he was sure he was not being followed he took to the great wagon road for ease of travelling, after spending a night in a clearing they set off early the following morning as they were anxious to get to Charlotte by the following day. After four hours travelling one of the two point riders galloped back to the Patriots pulling his horse up beside the Captain he asked him to call a halt, after the troop had dismounted he led the rider away from the rest.

"Now what ails you man?

"There has been a massacre up ahead; a small wagon train has been attacked by Indians, we think it was the same party as Arthur and the Rev came in with"

"Are there any survivors?

"We found none they have all been killed and scalped even the women and children"

"MY GOD! Will you go and send Arthur to me"

Arthur walked over to the Captain leading his horse by the bridle,

"You wanted me sir?

"Yes the point riders have found evidence of an Indian massacre; all the indications are that it is the same wagon train you came to Charlotte with"

"Are you sure, have there been any survivors?

"If you re-join the troop we will check it out"

By the time they were all mounted the remainder of the troop were aware of what had happened, and they set off at a steady trot towards the place where the massacre took place. The sight that greeted them was horrendous bodies were scattered all over the place men women and children had been murdered and scalped, all the wagons had been stripped of their goods and burned. The troop undertook the task of gathering the bodies and lining them up for Arthur to carry out the gruesome task of identifying them. Everybody was naked and it was obvious from the position of the female bodies that they had been raped, he recognised all that remained of the adults as the wild animals had been gorging themselves for several days. But he could not be sure that all the children were present. While he was identifying the bodies the remainder of the troop had been digging a shallow grave, the bodies were laid out in a row and Arthur had fashioned some small crosses from wood he salvaged from the burnt wagons. When the bodies were covered he placed a cross with the name scratched on it at the foot of each body, Archibald Armstrong, John Craig, George Gibson, John Dixon, and Sam Gray together they had travelled from Ulster to the new world for a better life and ended up with just a small plot in North Carolina. Captain Polk led the prayers for the dead, and all the militia men, regardless of religious beliefs joined in. The following morning the Captain addressed his men, it is obvious that this atrocity had been carried out by the Catawba Nation, several Indian tribes which had amalgamated together, the largest of which was the Cherokee, and they were fighting on the side of the loyalists who were rewarding them for every American patriot scalp. Some of the Patriots backwoods men had started looking for signs at first light and found the tracks of a large body of Indians leading a number of shod horses. Their tracks led towards Charlotte and it was well known that Nelsons mill which was just ten miles south of the village was occupied by loyalists and their Indian allies. This mill had been a thorn in the side of the patriots in the area around Charlotte for a long time but they had never been properly organised or had enough arms to do anything about it. The captain drew up a plan to eliminate this nest of loyalists and their Indian allies; he gathered the troop around him and laid out his plan Arthur and his platoon were to lead the attack as soon as it became dark in the meantime they must clean their guns and sharpen their pikes and axes. As the sun began to go down Arthurs ten volunteers travelled through the dense forest, by passing the mill until they were up stream, the men removed their boots and laid them on the bank with their gun and ammunition pouch, they would rely on their pikes which they had slung over their shoulder and their razor sharp axe tucked in their belt. They silently entered the water and began wading towards the giant mill wheel, Arthur was first to step on to the cross wooden pieces securing the outer rings of the wheel, as the wheel reached the highest point he just stepped off into the top room where the corn was ground. The other nine men followed him without incident; four of the men pikes at the ready positioned themselves at the top of the stairs the remainder got ready to slide down the chute and take the defenders from the rear. Just as it was getting dawn the four men quietly descended the stairs and quietly unbolted the main gate, when the Captain saw the gate swing open he charged, the residents were completely taken by surprise the attackers discharged their weapons then set to with their bayonets, as soon as the loyalists realised they were also being attacked from the rear they threw down their weapons and begged for quarter. At the rear of the mill was an enclosed area surrounded by a high wooden fence, ten men guarded the prisoners while the other forty burst into this area which was occupied by Indian warriors. Before the warriors were aware of what was going on the militia were into them with bayonet pike and axe they did not ask for quarter and none was offered, in less than thirty minutes twenty bodies lay strewn around the camp. The militia now searched the camp for personal effects belonging to the slaughtered members of the wagon train, numerous items such as jewellery and family heirlooms were loaded into their supply carts. Arthur took a couple of militia friends and started searching the tepees; he was almost finished when he entered the furthest one away and located the scalps hanging from a pole. As he was about to remove them he caught a movement out of the corner of his eye,

"Who's there" he shouted brandishing his axe.

"It's me Joseph Craig; have you any news of my family?

"Come out Joe where I can see you it's Mr. Patton"

Arthur recognised the fifteen year old as the son of John Craig the doctor,

I'm afraid I have no good news Joe your parents together the rest of the wagon train were massacred you are the only one still alive, the boy fell to his knees his body racked with sobs. Captain Polk had the militia round up the loyalists, and then he addressed them,

"You men are now prisoners of war and as such you will be taken to Lexington prison and kept there for the duration. However if each and every one of you will swear an oath never again to bear arms against the government of America I will release you to return to your families and farms".

James Moor spoke on behalf of the loyalists,

"We need to be left alone to decide which of the two options we wish to adopt"

The guards pulled back to allow them an opportunity to make a decision, there was much arguing and shouting among the loyalists after some time James Moor signalled that they had reached a decision and the Captain went forward to speak to him.

"We have reached a unanimous decision that we will return home and no longer take up arms in support of King George. If you draw up the paper we will sign it".

"I will draw up the paper forthwith; while I am doing this you will carry the bodies of the Indians into the fort and pile them in a heap.

The loyalists carried out the orders signed the paper and left the mill taking their dead and injured with them to their homes in the Martinborough district. The Captain now ordered a bag of black gunpowder to be brought from the supply wagon; the powder was sprinkled over the corpses, the floor and the walls of the mill, he led a trail of powder outside the building then set it alight, the militia retreated to a safe distance and watched as the mill burn to the ground.

That group of Indians will not find their happy hunting ground said Arthur with grim satisfaction. The following day they arrived back in Charlotte and Arthur took young Joe Craig to the manse, there he told the whole story to the Reverend Kerr and handed over the goods and chattels he had recovered from the Indians.

"Young Joe can stay here with my wife and I for as long as he wishes, I will speak to Liza tomorrow about getting him into school, we cannot leave our friends out there on the trail in a shallow grave, I intend to recover their bodies back here to Charlotte where they will be reunited with their scalps and buried in holy ground this will be the first burial service in my new Church"

The wagons set forth the following morning to bring back the bodies, a number of fully armed militia accompanied them, and on return they were reunited with their scalps and given a good Christian burial in the cemetery. The Reverend Kerr searched through their belongings for details of their families then sat down at his desk and wrote to their next of kin notifying them of their relative's demise. The little town of Charlotte developed a reputation as a good place for travellers to settle, few towns this far south could boast of having a church with a preacher and an excellent school for children of all religious denominations and ages. The law was administered by the Committee of Safety, and crime was almost unheard off. Large numbers of Loyalist farmers were abandoning their farms and moving north to seek the protection of the English army and navy. Most of the new arrivals were Farmers who were happy to grow crops of potatoes wheat and barley; many European countries were in the market for this produce, particularly France and Spain.

As the population of Charlotte grew funding soon became available to buy arms and ammunition for the militia, they now patrolled the outskirts of the town daily and Indian raids ceased, whole tribes were moving south and west leaving huge tracts of land freely available for the wagon trains arriving from the north to settle on.

Chapter 12 Sullivan Island

Alex spent the following week clearing up his affairs and saying his goodbyes; now that he was free, when the war ended he would begin the search for his beloved wife Elizabeth. True to his word James Crawford presented Alex with his captain's uniform in the South Carolina Artillery company, a fine brace of pistols with a quantity of ball and shot, he also presented him with a purse containing five golden guineas and the horse and tackle of his choice. It was early April 1776 and Alex threaded his way through thick forest following old Indian and animal tracks. The pistols in his belt were at half cock as he frequently encountered wolves and bears but he had no cause to use them, dressed in patriot uniform he was more concerned about meeting up with loyalist militia. For two nights he managed to secure board and lodgings in small hamlets along the path, on the third day he entered Charles Town. Alex rode his horse up Market Street until he came to a hostelry called the MERRY WIDOWS after stabling his horse he booked a room for the night. The town was teeming with South Carolina Militia and Regular soldiers, he had to get used to returning the many salutes from the lower ranks. After dinner that evening he entered the bar with the intention of having a good drink, this was the first bar he had frequented for many years. He had just downed his third whisky when the women he presumed was the Merry Widow herself come and joined him.

"Good evening captain we don't often have the pleasure of entertaining men from the artillery regiment I presume you are on the way to Sullivan Island"

"You are very observant Madame, how would a lady like you know about the different uniforms worn by American soldiers, you should be more careful about asking soldiers their destination there are loyalist spies are everywhere"

"My name is Mary Latimer better known as the Merry Widow, my husband was captain of a Privateer out of Charles

Town smuggling duty free goods from the Bahamas, he was intercepted by an English Man O War in seventeen seventy two and they hanged him and the entire crew, you will find no love for King George in this establishment"

"That's a sad story Mary, but a word of advice to you, these are difficult times and you should not ask a soldier where he is serving, however I will tell you that I hail from Ulster and my mother's people were Latimers".

They now moved to a table in the corner and continued their conversation, Alex told her about eloping with Lord Dawson's daughter and everything that had happened to him since. Mary listened to him carefully and told him that her deceased husband knew most of the ships captains operating the immigrant trade, when in port they always frequented her establishment, if Alex could supply her with information on the date of the voyage and the name of the ship and its captain she would make enquiries. She brought pencil and paper to the table and he wrote the name The John, into New

York arriving July 28th 1764 the captain was Luke Kiersted Mary gathered up the paper and deposited it in her ample bosom.

"The captain's name is vaguely familiar; I will start asking questions without delay"

Alex thanked her profusely; she reminded him they both came from Ulster with the name Latimer their families could well be related. He now asked if she would stable his horse and look after his saddle and bridle for the foreseeable future he would pay a month in advance.

"That will not be a problem "she said.

The following morning after a hearty breakfast Alex flagged down one of the many ammunition carts on their way to the fort on Sullivan's Island, the driver was not in uniform, he informed him that he worked for a private contractor whose job was to deliver guns and ammunition to wherever they were required by The South Carolina Artillery Company.

Alex observed that they progressed at a slow walking pace, the cart being pulled by two bullocks the track they were following had been turned into slimy mud by the hoofs of the animals. On arriving at the ammunition dump which was located underground Alex alighted, he enquired of the driver the name of his boss, the driver said it was his brother Thomas Mc Crea, as captain of the artillery Alex said he needed to meet with him urgently no later than the following day. He then set off to find the headquarters of the second South Carolina regiment, on entering he was met by a young second Lieutenant who looked like he was straight out of military academy he snapped to attention and gave a text book salute.

"What can I do for you Captain?

"I need to see Colonel Moultrie; my name is Captain Alex Williamson I am here to take command of the artillery".

"I will inform him straight away that you have arrived he has been waiting to meet you, we heard of your brave exploits at Moore's Creek it was a wonderful victory which made us all proud to be Americans"

He entered an inner office returning almost immediately.

"The Colonel will see you now" And he stood aside to let Alex past"

A middle aged man with long grey hair stood up from behind his desk and advanced towards him hand outstretched, Alex gave him an awkward salute and then shook his hand which was like leather, this was a man who had lived in the mountains for years trapping wild animals and fighting Indians in order to survive, he indicated a chair and said

"Tell me all about Moore's Creek it was a wonderful victory and filled us with the belief that we can take on the British and win".

Alex proceeded to give him a blow by blow account which lasted thirty minutes, when he had finished the Colonel said.

"Let's get down to business Alex we are desperately in need of your services, we have an assortment of some thirty cannon, they are mounted on wooden gun platforms secured with wooden spikes. At the moment they are manned by the army, who quite frankly are useless, but they are good patriots and keen to learn, at present the weather is too bad for the English navy to get into position to attack but we are not sure when the weather will change".

"First things first said Alex I need a good second in command I was impressed by your young Lieutenant can I have him?

"His name is Wilson he is another Ulster man, he will be a great loss to me, but when the British attack it will be the artillery doing most of the fighting so I must make the sacrifice. He shouted at the top of his voice Lieutenant

Wilson front and centre, and he marched smartly in snapping to a parade ground salute, Lieutenant I am assigning you to Captain Williamson he has asked for you, let him down and your father will hear about it from me.

"It will be an honour to work with the Captain",

Turning to Alex he said,

"How can I be of service sir?

"First you must find me an office preferably adjacent to the armoury, any room will do but I must have a desk and chair now off with you, they both saluted the Colonel and marched out into a wet windy day".

Alex mounted the ramparts and began his visual inspection of the ordinance, he had a pencil stub and a notebook in which he made notes, he paused to study the entrance to Charles Town harbour from the sea, noticing how narrow it was he concluded it would be very tight for large war ships to navigate. It was late afternoon when he had finished his inspection, and a private arrived with a message for him to join Bob Wilson in the armoury, when he arrived he was shown into a room which had been converted into an office he nodded his satisfaction to the Lieutenant and took his seat behind a large desk, indicating for him to sit opposite.

"Bob we have a tremendous amount of work ahead of us, please take notes first job is to recruit a company of men from the second brigade to reinforce the armoury, one direct hit from a cannon ball at the moment would send the lot sky high, they must reinforce the roof with timber then stack sand bags four feet deep on top. Next we must remove the cannon that we are not going to use, the two twenty six pound French cannon use too much powder to fire a large ball the required distance, the nine to twelve pound cannon will not do enough damage, we are going to standardise using the twenty five British eighteen pounders. These are quality pieces and will provide ample fire power, all other guns are to be removed from the ramparts and the eighteen pounders to be distributed evenly along the line, this will do for now you may schedule a further meeting for mid-day tomorrow"

As the dawn came up the following morning nine British war ships came over the horizon, Alex estimated they would have about three hundred cannon between them but not all will be able to come to bear at the same time. Thomas Mc Crea arrived to see him early morning,

"You wanted to see me Captain; I am contracted by the South Carolina legislature to move all weapons and material of war to wherever they are needed"

"Sit down Tom" he said indicating the chair opposite.

When he was seated Alex went on to explain the reasons why he asked for him to come.

"There are a number of things that concern me, but between us we will get to grips with them. Let me bring you up to date, nine British war ships have been sighted this morning heading for Charles Town, when they come in range will depend on the weather, I intend to use only the eighteen pounder cannon, without more time for training I anticipate firing about twelve hundred shot per day. Lieutenant Wilson will do a stock take and I want this number of ball to be in stock plus one day emergency supply. In the event we run short you will set up supply wagons pulled by fast horses I will need additional supplies of ammunitions delivered within one hour of you receiving our request. Can you meet these demands Tom?

"I can, and I will, it is up to us to keep the British out of Charles Town if they get Charles Town they will take the south"

"By noon tomorrow we should have completed our stock take in addition to the ammunition we will need one ammunition carriage per two guns, a rammer a sponge and a priming iron for each gun"

"You will have those by the end of the day" said Tom

After Tom departed Alex climbed up on the ramparts to see how the work was progressing, he didn't interfere as there were men scurrying about dismounting a gun from one carriage and mounting it on another. Glancing out to sea he could see the ships still fighting the storm, at present they were making no headway towards land. He descended back down to the armoury where he searched the stores for the tools required in any artillery battle. He was looking for a tool called a searcher this was used by the gunner to detect any cracks in the barrel, he found two standing up in a corner he carried them out to his office with two sponges. When Lieutenant Wilson reported back to him he was accompanied by an infantry sergeant who he introduced as Sergeant Andy Harper, Andy had asked to join the artillery as he knew that was where the action would be.

"I have just the job for you Sergeant, do you know what these are holding out the sponge and the searcher?

"I recognise the sponge but not the other thing"

"Come with me and I will show you how it works"

They found a cannon waiting to be secured in place and Alex first demonstrated the sponge, he then showed him how the searcher works by pushing it in the full length of the barrel he expanded it then slowly began to retract it, if it detects a crack it will snag and have to be released by the second handle. Every gun must be crack tested before it fires for safety reasons.

"This is an important job if a crack is not detected then the gun may explode killing the entire crew" said Alex.

It was now time to call for volunteers to transfer from the infantry into the artillery each gun would need one corporal to act as gun captain and five privates to operate it. Alex wanted to select the twenty five gun captains himself without delay as he wished training to begin immediately. Word that the artillery were looking for recruits soon spread, and the first twenty five corporals were appointed to their positions in day one. Their training began immediately and it soon became obvious that some of the volunteers would never reach the standard Alex set for an elite artillery company. The weak links were soon discovered and replaced with strong intelligent men capable of getting the last ounce of effort out of their gun crews; they were informed that the Royal Navy's fire power would be concentrated on destroying the forts defences. When the gun captains were fully trained in the art of cleaning and reloading their cannon they were each allocated their own gun and each corporal was instructed to appoint five of his best men to form his gun crew. It was the end of May when Alex called for a display of their proficiency; each gun will fire two blank rounds in front of Colonel Moultrie who will be timing the exercise. The men were positioned three on each side of the cannon each man holding his allocated tool, the corporal was responsible for the slow match which must be kept alight at all times, three of the privates were responsible for the rammer, the sponge, and two priming irons. After firing the blanks the guns recoil depended on the size of the shot, the private rammed the wet sponge down the barrel to extinguish any flames in it, it was his responsibility to supply a barrel full of clean water next to the gun carriage. The cannon was slightly raised to avoid the Cannon ball rolling out, firstly the gunpowder contained in a cloth was rammed down the barrel followed by the cannon ball, a wad of hay was then added to stop the cannonball rolling out, all hands were needed to pull the cannon up to its stops in battery position. The gun captain will align it on target, a pricker is used to puncture the charge then the corporal fires it by applying the quick match to the touch hole. Several of the guns were able to achieve a discharge every two minutes which pleased the officers, Alex had hoped for ninety seconds which is what the Royal Navy are capable of but the Colonel was delighted with the time his men had achieved. Tom McCrea had managed to supply twelve powder wagons which were now in position. Lieutenant Wilson had managed to convert them to store both powder and shot. It was now the middle of June and the weather was improving daily, the Royal navy ships were getting closer by the day it was now time to range the guns. He decided to fire seven guns at a time each one had a different range, he used the time remaining to choose their target area and carry out some practice shots, depending on the range each battery had a different size of the powder wad. At the last minute Tom Mc Crea delivered a load of grape shot which general Lee had captured. It was delivered to the battery in the middle of the line where it did good work demasting at least one British war ship. General Henry Clinton and Admiral Sir Peter Parker anchored near the entrance to Charles Town harbour in Five Fathom Hole an attempt to land infantry on long island proved unsuccessful as the water was two deep between it and Sullivan's Island. On June the seventh the British demanded surrender, but the patriots turned it down, the fifty gun h.m.s Bristol and Experiment together with six frigates opened fire on the fort, with little effect, their shot was ineffective due to the forts clever construction. The forts batteries opened fire, Alex had recognised FIVE FATHOM HOLE as being a likely anchorage and had his first battery with the best gunners zeroed in on it, almost immediately they found their range and started inflicting considerable damage. By midday Alex was worried about his ammunition and sent a rider to inform Mc Crea that he was desperate. True to his word the ammunition carts started to arrive pulled by fast horses, they arrived in the fort at full gallop and the ammunition was quickly distributed where it was needed most by the infantry. The naval war ships were sustaining an unacceptable amount of damage and Admiral Parker was considering withdrawal but General Clinton was for continuing the attack. Looking down from the fort Alex and the Colonel were pleased with the way the battle was going, suddenly he detected a problem with battery six which had stopped firing as he ran towards it he felt a heavy thud in his back which sent him flying down into the fort. Lieutenant Wilson saw the captain get hit and scrambled down the steep slope believing that he was dead, as he knelt beside him he heard a low moan of pain, he could see the deformity in his left shoulder and his left arm was missing above the elbow. He used his scarf as a tourniquet to slow the bleeding from what was left of his arm, then he flagged down an ammunition wagon, with the help of the driver he loaded Alex in the back,

"Will you take him to the dressing station at Mason's farm, as quick as you can and inform the medic that I have tied a tourniquet on his injured arm which must be released immediately".

The driver took off at a slow pace not wishing to add to Alex's discomfort, on arrival two orderlies unloaded him and got him inside on a bunk, seeing the seriousness of his injuries they sent for the M.D. On arrival he ordered the orderlies to place him on the table, he intended to remove the remains of the shattered arm while the patient was still unconscious, for the next two hours he cut away pieces of tattered flesh and made a neat cut in the bone with his saw. When he had finished and the wounds were dressed he got the orderlies to sit him up, he probed the disjointed shoulder when he was satisfied he placed one hand on his chest and the other behind his shoulder then with one sudden wrench he replaced the shoulder back in its joint. He ordered the orderlies to put him in a bunk near the door which was reserved for the dying, from past experience he knew that when Alex wakes up the shock from the pain he is in is likely to cause his heart to stop. Within a week he had developed a fever and was in and out of consciousness, after the first couple of weeks the surgeon no longer paid him a visit as he had other soldiers he felt he could save. Lieutenant Wilson and sergeant Harper visited him regularly but eventually they were posted up north were the fighting was at its fiercest and artillery men were desperately needed. At times the orderlies felt that Alex was rallying then the fever would take over again, he could be heard having a conversation with someone called Elizabeth his body deteriorated and he looked like a six year old child in the bunk. Then one morning, he opened his eyes and spoke to the orderly who immediately called for the surgeon, the surgeon examined Alex and said to the orderly,

"I don't believe it he may well survive, move him away from the door and give him some food"

When the patient was well enough to talk he asked the orderlies where his wife had gone to, the orderlies did not know what he was talking about, but he was adamant that she had been beside his bed holding his left hand it was then that they informed him he had no left hand.

Chapter 13 Mary Latimer

True to her word Mary Latimer had put the word around that she was trying to contact Captain Luke Kierstad, one day in June word reached her that he was below in the bar drinking with some of his shipmates. She recognised him immediately as he had sailed with her late husband on several occasions, she got her favourite seat in the corner and sent for him. After exchanging pleasantries they got down to business.

"Luke I am trying to trace the wife of a good friend of mine who is serving with the South Carolina Artillery on Sullivan's island, this lady travelled with you on the John from Newry Ireland, you berthed in New York August 64".

"I remember the voyage well it proved to be very profitable, it was without incident apart from the Royal Navy press gang boarding us and removing several of our young fit men, this was not an unusual occurrence in those waters".

"Captain Williamson was one of those men who were press ganged, and it is he who is currently fighting the British on Sullivan's Island, now he has never seen his wife since the day he was taken off the John; have you any recollection of her?

"It's nearly twelve years ago but I do have a vague recollection of a young woman unable to pay her passage because the British had shanghaied her man, the owners insisted on her being sold in the slave auction to cover the cost of her and her man's passage, the auction rooms in Wall Street New York should have a record of who bought her. I am leaving on the tide tomorrow with a load of tobacco for New York, and I will check the records in Wall Street and find out who the buyer was"

"If you would do that for me you would never have to pay for a drink in this establishment again, how long will it be before you return this way again?

"I shall be returning to Charles Town with a load of fertiliser in August and I hope to have some news for you then"

With that Luke returned to his companions and Mary retired to her rooms well satisfied with her achievements, the following morning she rode in her pony and trap to Sullivan's island, the battle was over and the Royal Navy ships had departed. She reported to the guard room an asked to speak to an artillery officer named Captain Williamson, the orderly officer on hearing her request invited her in,

"The Captain received a serious injury and was taken to the dressing station at Mason's farm; I have no further news on his condition".

As she had just passed the aid station on her way to the Island she decided to return there forthwith, when she got to the aid station the situation had calmed down and most of the patients were on the way to recovery. She was directed to Alex's bunk where she got the shock of her life, there before her eyes was a gaunt ghostly Skeleton of a man nothing like the man who had visited her establishment a couple of months past.

"Oh my God what has happened to you?"

"I had an argument with a British cannon ball and I came off worst, if you think I look bad now you should have seen me a month ago?

The surgeon had been told of Mary's arrival and appeared on the scene.

"Are you a relative? He asked

"We could be, his mother and I share the same name and we both come from Ulster".

"He is desperately in need of some good home nursing care, and decent food, he has made a remarkable recovery from being at deaths door".

Mary looked directly at Alex,

"I have spare rooms at the MERRY WIDOWS if you would like to come and stay with me, I have some news about Elizabeth which I will tell you later?

"I would be delighted to come and stay with you"

With that the surgeon called an orderly to come and help Alex to get dressed then they both left in the trap after Alex thanked the Surgeon and the orderlies for their kindness and excellent care. Back at the hostelry Mary found him a comfortable room and some civilian clothes that fitted him better than his uniform. The short journey had tired him out so he knew that a full recovery would take some time, he was determined that he would walk a fair distance each day in order to build his strength up. Mary told him about the Captain of the John visiting her and he was going to find out what happened to Elizabeth, he would be returning in August when he hoped to have more news. When Alex felt able he got his horse out of the stables and went for a ride, the loss of his arm made him feel very awkward, one side of his body appeared heavier than the other but he was determined to be ready to continue his search for Elizabeth when the Captain returned. It was near the end of August when Luke Kiersted turned up again at the Merry Widows; Mary sent a message for Alex to come and join them. He began by telling them that Elizabeth Williamson had been sold for Ten pounds sterling to a farmer named Arthur Patton from East Donegal Philadelphia. He had nothing more to tell them, apart from the facts that like him the Patton's were Presbyterians and he had heard tell of a Presbyterians church in East Donegal Township. Colonel Moultrie gave Alex a six month leave pass, after six months he was to report to the South Carolina artillery regiment, his health was almost back to normal, he had gained weight and felt he was ready to go searching for Elizabeth in Pennsylvania. Before he left he paid a visit to a branch of Gilmores bank which had recently opened in Charles Town, he presented both his and Grahams promissory notes and was requested to produce proof of his identity, he showed them the document freeing him from bondage signed by members of THE CONTINENTAL CONGRESS OF AMERICA, this was sufficient, and he was paid in gold coins to the value of one hundred pounds sterling. By the end of the week he was ready to leave having bought a pack mule which Mary loaded with supplies for the journey; he took half the money and left the remainder for her to put in her safe. At dawn the following day Alex set off north on his five hundred mile journey, he had arrived in America by sea and had no idea what lay ahead of him. His pistol and tomahawk were in his belt and his scalping knife was dangling on his chest secured by a cord round his neck. He had several rivers to cross ,some he could ford but others he would need to take the ferry, this was when he was at greatest risk from Tories. He set a reasonable pace for the animals; he dismounted every hour and walked for half an hour to give his mount a break. On both sides of the road were thick trees so he kept his eye out for a clearing near water to make camp, there were plenty of bears and wolves in the forest so he kept a fire burning all night, although it kept the animals at bay it put him at risk of an Indian attack. At least once a week Alex would meet a wagon train heading south for the Promised Land, he would seek out the wagon master and question him about a Presbyterian church in EAST DONEGAL Philadelphia, and the answer was always negative so he continued his journey. Five weeks passed and he crossed the border from Virginia into Pennsylvania, from then on he would make enquiries from any settlement he came across. He was directed towards Lancaster which was the largest town in the district; there was a lot of military travelling in the opposite direction to him. He made several attempts to find out what was going on but nobody would stop and talk to him, as he approached Lancaster he encountered more and more British soldiers. As he entered the town he was stopped and questioned by armed guards, the missing left arm roused their suspicions that he was a patriot soldier and he was escorted to the company office. Having searched his belongings they found his uniform and his papers releasing him from bondage signed by THE CONTINTAL CONGRESS, now that they knew he was an ex criminal they demanded to know what crime he had committed.

"Sheep stealing", He lied.

A young lieutenant had entered the guard room and taken charge of the questioning.

"We don't believe you, why would The Continental Congress sign your release papers and appoint you to the rank of Captain; we have apprehended you wearing civilian clothes and have every right to put you on trial as a spy before we hang you, put him in a cell corporal until we get to the bottom of this".

Alex remained in custody for several weeks, before being paraded before the company commander and two senior officers, they listened to the evidence of arrest before finding him guilty and sentencing him to be hanged in one week, this gave him time to make his peace with god. On returning to his cell he requested permission to see a Presbyterian minister, the nearest meeting house was in East Donegal and the minister was sent for immediately. Two days later he arrived on horseback and they were left alone in the cell, Alex spent an hour explaining to the Reverend what brought him to Lancaster and that he was a captain in the American army. Jim Ward was a senior elder when the Rev Kerr set off to the south leading a wagon train; he took charge of the parish until a new preacher could be found. Jim knew all the families who left and yes there was a farmer named Patton who was accompanied by two women and two children. He could remember them well, one of the women Margaret was Patton's wife and the other woman was called Lizzy Williamson. They took the Great Wagon Road south and that was the last he had heard of them. Alex was delighted to hear that Elizabeth was alive, now he had to get out of prison and go find her. Jim informed him that the 9th Pennsylvania regiment were poised to attack Lancaster and he doubted the British would try to defend it, he needed to hold out for another twenty four hours. That night Jim Ward with fifty minute men and some local militia attacked the cells, the six guards thinking it was the 9th Penn regiment fled without firing a shot. The militia had brought a horse and mule to the front door, Alex found his belongings in a cupboard loaded them on the mule then after thanking Jim mounted his horse and set off south in the darkness. To avoid the British sentries Alex kept to the deepest part of the woods, it was so dense in places he had to dismount and lead the animals by the head. When dawn appeared he sought out a small clearing, having tethered the animals he lay down to get some badly needed sleep. He was awakened by someone kicking at his feet; he recognised the men's uniforms as soldiers belonging to the 9th Penn regiment.

"Get on your feet barked the sergeant in charge, who are you?

"Alex Williamson, captain in the south Carolina Artillery".

"Why are you dressed in civilian clothes, and riding a British horse you're a spy aren't you?

 "No! I was a prisoner of the British, they found me guilty of spying and sentenced me to hang tomorrow morning, but I escaped with the help of some American minutemen who came to my rescue".

"You're a spy and as we are about to attack Lancaster tomorrow I do not have time to argue with you".

A corporal who had heard the entire conversation then butted in,

"Sergeant he may be telling the truth we should wait until we have had time to check out his story"

"Where do you suggest we should keep him, we have no secure prison accommodation and the attack begins at first light tomorrow, fetch me a rope"

With that the corporal rode off to find the quartermaster, and collect a rope, he had to explain what he wanted it for and on hearing the reason the quartermaster handed it over. He then had some reservations so he walked to the commanding officers tent and informed him sergeant Davis who was known to be headstrong was about to hang a man as a spy, without checking out his story. When he arrived with the rope Alex was mounted on his horse facing the tail, a private soldier held the horse by the head. After creating a noose the rope was thrown over a stout branch and the noose placed over Alex's head the other end of the rope was fastened to an adjacent tree. As the sergeant was about to signal for the horse to be led away there was a commotion among the watching soldiers and into the clearing rode the commanding officer.

"If you are satisfied this man is a spy then by all means hang him, we have more important things to attend to, with that he looked at the condemned man's face and let out a roar".

 "STOP! Alex-Alex Williamson is that you?

"Alex looked at the commanding officer in utter disbelief, is it you James O'Hanlon"

"One of you remove that rope of my friend's neck, as for you Davis next time I see you if you are still wearing those stripes I will have you court-martialled".

Both men dismounted and shook each other vigorously by the hand,

"Alex mount up and follow me back to my command post, I want to hear all about you and how you come to be here".

Colonel O'Hanlon had a large tent in the middle of his regiment's billets, as it was a fine day they sat outside with a jug of poteen and told each other their stories. James told how he escaped the hangman in Ireland by the skin of his teeth, he signed on as a sailor on an emigrant ship using a false name, when the ship docked in Boston he jumped ship and joined the patriot movement. He was a natural leader and rapidly rose through the ranks; he now commanded one of the most successful regiments in the American army. If everything went to plan he intended to rout the British tomorrow and chase them out of Lancaster. Now it's your turn Alex, you tell me your story, it took nearly an hour to relate the full story to James, junior officer kept interrupting asking for orders, when he had finished the Colonel had some comments to make. He told Alex the story all Ulster men knew that a wagon train from East Donegal had been ambushed by Indians just outside Charlotte and there was only one young survivor. Next he informed him he had eight four pounder cannon and no one trained to use them properly, he asked Alex to take charge of the battery and support the attack on the morrow. He agreed without hesitation and the battery officer was sent for as soon as he was introduced to Alex his eyes lit up as he had heard of his exploits at Moore's creek and Sullivan's island. Alex donned his uniform and accompanied the battery officer to inspect the four pounders, the lieutenant ordered the gun crews to attend their cannon and Alex carried out an inspection. Each gun had two ammunition boxes one on each side of the gun, the limbers were parked several yards behind the guns ready when the cannon were loaded on them to became a mobile weapon which could be moved rapidly by two horses to any part of the battlefield. The ammunition wagons filled with case shot and powder were parked nearby ready to follow the guns; they were pulled by a single horse. After issuing some orders Alex returned to the command post he asked to see the order and position of the attack. James laid out the map on the table showing the position of the soldiers when the attack would start, Alex spent some time studying the map then pointed out that because of the density of the trees his guns would be of little use. He pointed to a hilly area to the left of the town and asked permission to move the guns there, this position would enfilade the British lines, and by raising the gun barrels to their maximum height he could rain down grape shot on their lines without the trees blocking the shot. The Colonel agreed without hesitation, and Alex got the troop ready to move at nightfall, two men would ride on each limber and one man on the horse pulling the ammunition wagon, a further twenty men were to get rations and move towards the high country. Alex also drew some rations and set off immediately to get in position for when the cannon arrived, to avoid being discovered the limbers took a wide route and the first guns arrived about midnight eight gun positions had already been marked out and when in position the limbers were removed each gun was loaded and the barrel raised to its maximum height, the case shot could be expected to travel two to three hundred yards and on exploding would send small jagged pieces of metal in all directions at tremendous velocity. The patriot army started their attack at first light, the British were waiting for them and they found it hard going, all eight canons were zeroed into the British line of defence when Alex gave the order to fire. The defenders were completely taken by surprise as shells rained down on them from on high exploding when they came into contact with the trees or the ground sending out shrapnel in a wide arc dozens of British soldiers died in the first salvo. The next order to the guns was to fire when ready, the untrained gunners took between one and three minutes to reload depending on their abilities, as the next salvos came in quick succession the defenders broke and took to their heels followed by the 9th regiment. Having cleared the British out of Lancaster James called a halt to the pursuit and set up a defensive line in preparation for a counter attack, he is now receiving many reports of a lack of ammunition and he had no emergency stock to replenish the deficiency. There was a huge celebration among the soldiers who were not on duty that night; the intelligence officers were reporting that the defeated British were boarding their ships in the docks prior to moving north. James and Alex spent the evening with a jug of homemade Irish whisky, the Colonel was expecting orders to replenish stores then move north in pursuit of the enemy. Alex pointed out he was an officer on sick leave from the South Carolina Artillery company so could not accompany the 9th, he must return to his regiment immediately. James gave him a letter commending him for his action in the liberation of Lancaster and two days later he set off south his horse and mule having been returned to him with a month's supplies.

Chapter 14 Growing up

The twins were going on fifteen, and as lovely as their mother was at that age, with Lizzy and Margaret now fully occupied with the school, teaching children in the day and learning adults to read and write in the evening. Lizzy spent a lot of time interpreting property deeds for the farmers, these documents were in Latin and she was the only person who had received a classical education. In addition to helping out in the school Margaret was assisting young Joe Craig now fourteen to attend the sick and injured citizens of Charlotte, he had learned a lot about healing and medicine from his father and fortunately for him his father's medical books had survived the massacre. The twins were good workers, they kept the Church and the Manse spotlessly clean as well as looking after the garden fruit trees and shrubs. They fed and milked the animals and when required they could kill and butcher a pig or a lamb, they were both good shots and often returned from a visit to the woods with a deer or other wild animal for the stewing pot. Arthur Patton had not been home for several months and Margaret was worried sick about him, rumour had it that Charles Town had fallen to the British and their troops were advancing north, the American continental army and militia had taken up defensive positions outside Camden and a battle was inevitable. It was nearly midnight at the end of August when a knock came on the door of the manse Fiona opened it and Arthur stood there totally exhausted and a bloody bandage wrapped around his right hand. She beckoned him in and went to get Margaret out of bed, after hugging him she led him through to the extension they had built at the back for treating the sick and disabled.

"Fiona get Joseph down here, Louise make some food and a drink of hot coffee"

With that she began to unravel the bandage on his hand, Young Craig arrived almost immediately.

"Here let me do that it looks nasty, what happened Mr Patton"

"A backfire the barrel of my gun got two hot and it backfired injuring my right hand I think it looks worse than it is, we lost the battle of Camden and the British are in hot pursuit if they catch me here you will all be in trouble, just patch my hand up give me some food and I will be on my way"

"You are going nowhere until you have had some rest" said Margaret.

Lizzy took the girls into their bedroom.

"Now you will both get dressed and take up a position in the trees at the edge of town Fiona you are the best climber so you will find a tree that gives you a good view down the trail, if you spot the British you will get back here post haste to warn us, now I don't have to tell you you're uncles life is in your hands don't let us down"

"We won't" they both said together.

Back at the house Joe had finished dressing Arthur's hand.

"Your hand has been badly burned but it will heal in a couple of weeks if you keep it clean"

"It feels much better already young man, your father would have been very proud of you"

Lizzy retired to the twin's bed leaving Margaret and Arthur alone, it was midday the following day when he was ready to leave, the girls had returned to say goodbye. They advised him that they had seen Captain Polk and a number of his militia men heading towards the captains house.

"Well that is where I am must go"

He hugged and kissed the girls before taking his leave. Rumour soon spread that General Cornwallis was on his way to Charlotte at the head of his troops, and word came from Arthur that they had been ordered to slow his advance by defending the town. On hearing this Lizzy and Margaret closed the school and removed the desks, they gathered half a dozen good pine tables which they scrubbed clean and placed inside ready to receive casualties. Joe Craig arrived to inform them he was joining the militia, he wanted to fight, nothing the women could say would make him change his mind. Margaret went to the Polk house to see the captain but she was informed that Major William Davie had arrived in town to take charge of the defence. She was escorted into his office where she explained that young Joseph Craig was the only physician in the town, they had set up an aid station and were desperately in need of his services but he had decided to join the militia and fight. Without a moment's hesitation he sent for Private Craig and ordered him to report to the aid station immediately, he pointed out to Joe that he had one hundred and fifty fighting men but no one to attend to the wounded. He was reluctant to leave his comrades but the Major pointed out that this was just a delaying tactic not a battle, when it got too hot he planned to pull out towards Salisbury. Margaret and Joe returned to the school house together where they continued with their preparation to receive casualties.

"Mrs Patton, what will I do if someone needs an amputation, I don't think I can do it?

"Course you can Joe the twins have volunteered to be nurses if they can overcome their fear of nursing wounded men you can amputate a limb".

Fiona high in her perch was first to spot the British and she hurried up East Trade Street to inform Major Davie, he quickly positioned his hundred and fifty riflemen behind a low wall in front of the post office and waited for the loyalist troops led by Major Hanger. When the British were one hundred yards away he ordered his men to stand up and open fire the loyalist taken completely by surprise fell back in disarray. Major Hanger quickly rallied his men and advanced on the patriots. Faced by overwhelming odds they fell back firing as they went. Two of the patriots were seriously wounded and were carried on makeshift stretchers through the trees towards the aid station, Captain Graham had several serious sabre wounds to his thighs and head he was not expected to survive, Private Johnsons ankle had been shattered by a musket ball and on examining him Joes worst fears were realized, if he was to save him he would have to remove the leg below the knee. The twins fetched and boiled water and when the time came to amputate they pushed down on a shoulder each, the boy was not much older than them and as he screamed the tears ran down their cheeks. Young Craig used his father's tools he cut through the skin and flesh with his knife then using his saw severed the bone, he performed at breakneck speed as he was afraid the patient would die of shock. On completion Margaret took over and dressed the wound Joseph had cauterised the wound with a red hot iron and the bleeding had almost stopped. Mean time Lizzy had dressed the captains wounds as best she could it would be some time before they would know if he would live or die. Four more young soldiers turned up with minor wounds one had a deep sabre wound in his buttock and when ordered to remove his drawers he looked at the twins, his face was flushed red. When he did get up the courage to remove them the girls did not help, they burst out laughing and their mother banished them to the well for more water. Only the captain and the amputee were kept under treatment the other four were returned to duty it had been a hectic time but the women were satisfied with their efforts, the twins had managed to overcome their shyness and developed from young girls to young women. The following day the two invalids were moved into the loft in the manse and the schoolhouse was restored to its former use, the British were now in full control of Charlotte and the fighting moved north towards Salisbury. It was two days later in the early evening when the family had finished their evening meal and were saying their prayers before retiring for the night; a loud knock came on the door. Fiona answered it and standing there, was a young British army officer, on observing her he swept his tricorn hat from his head with a flourish and gave her a stiff bow. She could only stare; she had never in all her life seen a more handsome young man he was dressed in a short red jacket secured with silver buttons, with white cross belts, and a sword with a silver hilt hung from his waist.

"Pardon the intrusion Miss but I have been sent here by Lord Cornwallis to seek out a Mrs Elizabeth Williamson"

"Fiona could only manage a whisper; I will fetch her you wait there".

She made her way into the kitchen where her mother was sitting,

"There is a British soldier at the door asking to see you mother do you think they know about the aid station? I'm afraid for you".

"Fiona you're talking nonsense if they knew do you think they would only send one soldier, now go and show him into the parlour and I will join him as soon as I have tidied myself up"

She went back to the front door her knees trembling,

"Follow me", and she led him into the parlour.

A few minutes later her mum joined them, noticing Fiona standing there staring at the young soldier she ordered her back to the kitchen, she then took a seat.

"Now then young man, how can I help you?

"Firstly I need to confirm that you are the right person that his lordship sent me to contact, prior to your marriage were you Elizabeth Dawson daughter of Lord Dawson of Dartrey in the county of Monaghan Ireland.

"That is correct"

"Then his Lordship would be honoured if you would attend on him on the morrow as he has some information he wishes to convey to you"

"Four o'clock would suit me as I have my pupils to teach, I believe he has taken up residence in Captain Polk's house"

"He has and I'm sure that will be fine, he will be looking forward to seeing you"

With that Elizabeth called Fiona to see the Lieutenant out; she stood in the doorway watching his fine upright military gait until he was out of sight. The following afternoon she chaperoned her mother on her visit to Lord Cornwallis, to her delight the young officer opened the door to them, he bowed to Elizabeth and looked directly at Fiona causing her to blush furiously. On entering his Lordships private quarters he jumped to his feet and hurried to meet them.

"Elizabeth I would have known you anywhere you are the spitting image of your mother and your daughter is the image of both of you. Edward take the young woman for a walk in the garden, you will stay in sight of the sentries I am not having the young lady compromised".

Elizabeth perched herself on the chaise lounge and accepted a glass of sherry from his Lordship, she noted he was rather portly the appearance of a man who enjoyed his food and wine, he had a kindly face which tended to put you at your ease.

"When your father knew I was to take command of his Majesty's armies here in North America he asked me to seek you out and beg you to return home, as he is a personal friend of King George I resolved to make every effort to obey him, on hearing of a school teacher here in Charlotte called Elizabeth Williamson from Ulster I sent young Edward Murray-Saunders to check you out. Before going any further it is my sad duty to inform you that your dear mother passed away in Nov 64, shortly after hearing you had married a farm hand and departed Ireland, she never recovered from the news"

Elizabeth was devastated at the news of her mother's death, more so as she was the cause of her demise, she was inconsolable for several minutes. When she recovered her composure his Lordship coughed gently, I'm afraid I have more bad news Your Ladyship, I have recently received a signal from the admiralty informing me of the death of Lord Dartrey, as you are his only child his solicitors are desperate to get in touch with you in order to settle his affairs. The title and family seat has passed to your nearest male relative Lord Richard Dawson but your father has left you various legacies including a large tract of land here in North America. I am returning to England in a couple of days as my beloved wife Jemima is hovering at deaths door and I wish to be with her at the end, you may accompany me on a naval ship of the line".

"I shall avail myself of your kind offer but first I need to make arrangements for the twins to be looked after" said Elizabeth.

"The day after to 'morrow I will send a coach for you in the forenoon, our ship is lying at anchor in Charles town harbour".

At that Elizabeth rose and went in search of Fiona who was reluctant to leave the company of her dashing soldier, the fact he was on the Loyalist side in the war did not trouble her. On returning to the manse she gathered Margaret and the twins together in the kitchen and explained what had transpired with Lord Cornwallis, they all hugged her and sympathised at the loss of her parents. Margaret agreed she would look after the twins while their mother returned to Ireland to settle her affairs it was anticipated it would take her about four months. Fiona raised her objections to her mother travelling unchaperoned and after a lengthy discussion it was agreed she could travel with her mother. Louise raised no objections she had become very attached to Joseph Craig and enjoyed working with him as his nurse; everybody agreed they made a lovely young couple. True to his word his Lordship sent a four seater coach to pick up the ladies then he and his aide joined them before setting off for Charles Town, they were protected by a platoon of cavalry on the journey. On boarding the warship the ladies were allocated an officers cabin, all four passengers dined at the captain's table every night, Elizabeth could not help comparing the journey home to the voyage on the John travelling to America. After dinner Fiona and Lieutenant Edward Murray-Saunders strolled around the deck to the amusement of the sailors. At first they had reservations about women on board, the superstitious men among them thought they would bring bad luck to the ship. Elizabeth joined in the after dinner discussions with the men it quickly became obvious that her sympathies were with the Patriots in America, his Lordship had to grudgingly admit that he had a sneaky admiration for a bunch of farmers and men of divers other occupations who had taken on his highly trained army and held their own. When they finally sailed into

Southampton they took their leave of the ship's captain and took their seats in a carriage which had been sent from Brome Hall Suffolk to bring the General home. They spent a night in London prior to continuing to the hall, the following day. Jemima Jones the general's wife was not well enough to meet them as she was confined to her bed; Elizabeth paid her respects to her later after the general had enjoyed his reunion. His lordship had very kindly put his carriage at her disposal to travel with Fiona to Liverpool where they would catch the mail packet to Dublin. The lieutenant travelled to Liverpool with them and when they arrived he said his farewell to Fiona and they both cried as they parted company. When on board the packed ship they went below to their cabin, it was at least an hour before Fiona was capable of holding a conversation with her mother. The following day they descended on to the dock, word had been sent by mail of their intended arrival and they looked for a carriage. Elizabeth spotted Bertie Millar with a carriage, he was eighteen years older but she recognised him instantly, he spotted her and rushed to meet them and directed the porter to load the luggage in the boot, then he helped the ladies to board the carriage before heading off north to Dartrey. There had been considerable improvements to the road since she left, and the trees had been cleared back from the road making it more difficult for Tories to surprise and ambush travellers. They rested overnight and changed horses in Carrickmacross before travelling on the following day. They arrived at the Castle in the middle of the day, her cousin Richard dashed down the steps and hugged her in a tight embrace, welcome home Your Ladyship we have been so anxious for your safety on the journey Elizabeth returned his embrace before introducing him to Fiona. The next few weeks were hectic as she and her cousin waded through a mountain of documents, her father had left her 600 acres of prime farm land in the Cumberland valley Tennessee, she had a number of properties and townlands in Ireland which she sold unseen to her cousin for £50,000 in return she purchased the freehold of Alex's parents farm in Derrycrenard, her cousin refused any payment for it. She spent days in Martins solicitors in Monaghan town sorting through the transfer of property and deeds in to her cousin's name. Finally she made time to take Fiona to meet her grandparents, on meeting when Elizabeth entered they curtsied to her and addressed her as My Lady; she threw her arms around Alex's mother.

"Shush now you are my mother now, and it is I who must show you respect"

Fiona loved her granny although she worked hard on the farm she still retained the posture and manners of an English lady, she was unsure of her grandfather as she could not understand a word he said in his broad scotch accent, but she could not mistake the warmth of the hug he gave her. When they were ready to leave Elizabeth gave him the deeds to the farm he looked at them then handed them to his wife she sat down before reading them and immediately understood what the document were. She then explained to Robert their meaning he fell to his knees taking Elisabeth's hand and smothering it with kisses, Fiona started to cry and her grandmother had to comfort her. Granny now pulled a chest from under the kitchen table and extracted a letter, handing it to her daughter in law she said it's from Alex; she took the letter her hands trembling.

"Do you mind if I take it home to read, I would prefer to be alone"

"Certainly not child, you may keep it"

Elizabeth held it to her lips, the tears were streaming down her face, and Fiona threw her arms around her she too was crying, when they got their emotions under control they left to return to Dawson Grove.

When she got home Elizabeth went straight to her bedroom clutching the letter in her hand her daughter did not follow her, feeling it best to leave her alone. The letter was in a beautiful hand she did not recognise, it had been written by a woman called Mary Latimer at a time Alex was in hospital recovering from the loss of his left arm, as another Ulster person with the name Latimer she had befriended him and promised to help him locate Elizabeth. The letter told how he missed his beautiful wife so much that at times he fell into a deep despair of ever finding her. He would not give up looking for her until the day he died. Other parts of the letter dealt with the loneliness of missing his family and Ulster. She went skipping down the stairway where her daughter was waiting.

"He's alive, your father is alive and looking for us we must return without delay"

She began putting pressure on Martins solicitor to transfer the deeds of the land in America into Alex's name as under their law women were not allowed to own property. In the meantime she decided to purchase some prize cattle, and pedigree horses, she knew if Alex decided to start a cattle ranch he would want to improve the American stock. The person at the castle who was in charge of ensuring that only the finest animals were bred there was Tom Latimer; he was a cousin of her husband. With his help she selected two prize Hereford bulls and two hunter stallions; these two horses were favoured by the best riders during the fox hunting season. She asked Tom if he would like to accompany the animals on their journey to America, her cousin Richard was reluctant to let him go but after some persuading he gave them his blessing. Elizabeth and Fiona spent a whole day saying goodbye to their relatives and friends and on the eve of their departure to everyone's surprise Lieutenant Murray-Saunders turned up at the castle. Fiona flew to his side and he put his arm around her and addressed Elizabeth,

"Your ladyship I have resigned my commission in the army and would like your permission to take Fiona for my bride, I am a man of independent means and well able to support her"

"Edward in the last couple of weeks we have discovered that her father is still alive and looking for us, it is her father who must give his blessing to your betrothal and in order to get that you must return with us to Charlotte"

"Nothing would please me more your Ladyship when shall we leave?

"My daughter and I are leaving for Dublin in the morning to arrange passage; it would please us if you would accompany our new stockman Tom as the animals in his care are very valuable and he may require protection"

Her cousin Richard accompanied the ladies to Dublin the following day, they stayed the night with his brother a prominent banker in the city, the following day the two brothers visited the White Star Line and arranged passage for four people and four animals the bank paid all the costs and they received the finest accommodation. Simon and Tom would travel with the animals; the shipping line arranged all fodder and water for the journey. One week later after saying goodbye to her cousins Elizabeth and her party departed on the long voyage to Charles Town South Carolina.

Chapter 15 Warriors Path.

Alex headed south on the Great Warrior Path, his pack horse was well supplied with all the essentials for a long journey. By now the road was well travelled with immigrants heading south for the free land in the Carolinas, he encountered numerous drovers herding cattle and pigs, at night the animals were herded into makeshift pens in the woods were they could feed on the abundant green grass. Most nights he spent in different saloons-hotels, he enjoyed the company, and also the drinking and playing cards, when he arrived in Winchester Virginia he felt like he was back home in Ulster, the people spoke English but some of the older people spoke a rich Scots Gaelic, good quality Poteen was available in most of the saloons it was brewed high up in the Appalachian mountains by the immigrant Irish. The inhabitants were anti British to the core; they remembered the rack rents in their homeland where decent families were being got put out of their farms to accommodate the absent landlords huge flocks of sheep. Alex decided to stay a second day to give his animals a rest after feeding them as he was walking back to the saloon he was accosted by a young man in the uniform of a corporal in the artillery who gave him a snappy salute, "Captain Williamson sir can I have a word with you".

"How do you know who I am? Explain yourself"

"Colonel O'Hanlon sent me to find you he knew you were travelling south and sent me after you, there are not many one armed artillery captains on the road. He will arrive here tomorrow with the 9th Lancaster regiment followed by his baggage train and artillery battery, you are ordered to await his arrival here"

"I appreciate he may want my help with the artillery but I have other more important business to a attend to"

"He thought you might be uncooperative so he authorised me to arrest you and request the town marshal to lock you up until he arrived".

"How were you planning on doing that Corporal? Said Alex fingering the pistol in his belt"

With that the young soldier raised his right hand high and six fully armed infantry men appeared with bayonets fixed.

"Alex gave a hearty laugh, come on you guys we are all on the same side put your guns away, if it is that important of course I will wait for the Colonel will you take my word for it Corporal"

"Your word is good enough for me Captain; perhaps we can have a drink together later?

It was three days later when the 9th Lancaster's bivouacked on the outskirts of Winchester, the Colonel sent a dispatch rider to request that Alex report to him in his h.q without delay. He presented himself within the hour and when the two men had settled down with a jug he requested to know what all the urgency was about.

"Alex at my request you have been transferred to the 9th under my command, as from now you are in command of all our artillery, it would appear we have Gen Cornwallis trapped in Yorktown with much superior forces to him. He may try to escape across the York River I have been allocated the task of ensuring his soldiers do not cross the half mile of water separating Yorktown, and Gloucester point on the opposite shore. When our baggage train and artillery arrive tomorrow we will give them two days to rest, then we will proceed to Gloucester point. This could be the big battle that ends the war, for the first time we have them outnumbered, with a mixture of American and French soldiers under the command of General Washington. Our part in the battle will be vital and we must prevent the British crossing the York River"

"I promise you Colonel the artillery will not let you down, by the time we join battle I will have a battery able to perform to the highest standards"

The two men drank a toast to victory then retired for the night. Alex was waiting on the parade ground the following morning when the artillery battery began to arrive, the gunners recognised him and had already been informed that he would be taking over command. The horses were unharnessed and led to some good grass nearby where they were hobbled and left to graze. Their commanding officer called a meeting of all gunners and n.c.os he had just received an order from the Colonel that Gen Washington had ordered that all American artillery pieces were to be painted light blue in honour of their French allies. A large body of civilian painters were standing by with the materials to begin, guns limbers and powder wagons were painted in six hours. And one day later the paint was dry enough for the guns to be handled, first job was to clean and crack test the weapons before practising loading and unloading. All the wheels were removed cleaned and packed with bear grease; the wheels which were made of elm or beach were checked for any cracks or distortion. The Colonel had the 9th drilling and practising their shooting skills continually; he was aware what lay ahead and wanted his men at their fittest. After a week's hard training the Colonel called a meeting with his officers and senior n.c.os, they paraded in front of his tent and he addressed them.

"Gentlemen I have to 'day received orders from General Washington, he and his French counterpart intend to launch an all-out attack on the British at the beginning of October, the British have the York River at their backs and may attempt to cross the half mile expanse of water to Gloucester Point and from there make their escape north. The loyalists have already established a small defensive military force at the point to cover the army's retreat, our job is to destroy that garrison and deny the loyalists a means of escaping, are there any questions?

"Sir Can you tell us which regiment we will be up against and what is their strength?

"I believe this force is made up mainly of a mixture of British regular regiments, we will be evenly matched but they may have been reinforced by the time we arrive, are there any more questions?

Nobody asked any more question so they were given their order for marching, the mounted 9th regiment would lead off followed by the artillery with their powder wagons, and they would be followed by the baggage train and ambulances. Their journey was taking them south east over little used Indian trails, the leading troops were widening the path to allow the guns and wagons to negotiate the narrow uneven trail. The scouts who were mainly mountain men travelled two days ahead of the main army; these men killed large quantities of fresh meat and left them hanging from the trees out of reach of predators. When the army reached Saguda the Colonel called a halt and all the horses were checked for lameness and illness, Alex had the guns cleaned and made ready for going into action. The scouts reported that the

British were well entrenched at the Point, and they had observed some boats ferrying food across to General Cornwallis whose men where near starvation. One of the scouts drew a map for Alex showing him the best vantage point to locate his artillery; he would have a clear view of the fortifications without too many trees blocking his view, he decided to scout this position for himself and was delighted with it. When night fell he led his artillery through the trees to the selected point, the limbers were removed and the ammunition boxes filled and ready. Eight buckets of water were carried and one placed beside each of the guns for the sponges, Alex checked that the powder was dry and in good condition, then he had the guns camouflaged with brush before he reported to Colonel O'Hanlon that he was ready. Later that day the whole company was formed up and addressed by the Col.

"Men of the 9th Lancaster's tomorrow I intend to attack Col Tarleton, this man is a butcher, he ignored an offer of truce from the Patriots at Waxhaw and ordered their destruction this was a crime and we are going to punish him and his legion of British and Scots loyalist for what they did to our compatriot's"

He dismissed the parade and invited Alex to join him in his tent.

"Captain I want you to open fire with all your cannon at first light, the British are unaware that we are camped here in the trees just five hundred yards from their fortifications. I anticipate Tarleton will make a full scale attack to try to put your artillery out of action, so I will attempt to ambush them at the Hook, we will give no quarter as we can expect none from him, and with the element of surprise on our side we should prevail, I do not anticipate many casualties. We have been reinforced by elements of the Mecklenburgh militia true patriots who will fight till they drop; they are accompanied by a medical team who have set up a hospital in Captain John Chisolm's ranch house"

"Colonel we will win, General Washington is depending on us to make sure the British do not cross the York River; with their retreat cut off he believes they will have no option but to surrender then with Cornwallis and his army in captivity the loyalists will find it impossible to continue with the war."

"I agree with your observations Alex, now we will call it a night as we have a big day tomorrow, God bless you and your men"

Alex mounted his horse and made his way through the trees up to his own lines, on arrival he assembled his gunners and arranged six men to sleep by each gun, very few of them slept that night and as daylight approached they removed the brush and manned their weapons. Four of the cannon were loaded with shrapnel and caseshot destined to explode ten feet of the ground spraying metal shards over a wide area, the other four armed with roundshot whose function was to destroy the fortifications. Alex checked the sighting of all the guns he then gave the order to fire at will. The loyalist mounted infantry were queuing up at the cookhouse for their breakfast when all hell broke loose, cannon shells were exploding in the air above them, mowing down men and horses while solid shot bounced along the ground creating holes in their defences. Colonel Tarleton rushed from his tent with his orderlies, he ordered his bugler to sound the call to arms, the loyalists grabbed their weapons and horses and assembled at a blind spot behind the fortification here they were out of range of the cannon. The scouts pointed to the heights were the guns were located and Tarleton led his Scotch highlanders towards them at full gallop. They headed for a crossroads called The Hook where they could turn right and attack the cannon from the rear. As they made their turn they were hit by the joint forces of the 9th and the militia total confusion ensued some of the highlanders put up a gallant fight but others wanted to surrender. O'Hanlon spotted Tarleton in his green jacket and white pants and fought his way towards him when he was in earshot he shouted above the din Colonel you murdered innocent men at Waxhaw, make your peace with God as now I am going to kill you. The two men came together with a crash swinging their sabres at each other's head; an unhorsed highlander observing the fight between the two Colonels used his dirk to slit the throat of O'Hanlon's horse leaving him on foot. The highlander then attacked him with his claymore; a militia man spotted the danger and split his skull open with his tomahawk. Tarleton seeing O'Hanlon on foot galloped his horse at him but he sidestepped the horse and slit his belly open as he went past, both men were now on foot and evenly matched with the sword, as the battle raged around them they tried to gain the upper hand on each other, Tarleton was being forced backwards when he slipped on his horses guts which covered the ground. Quick as a flash O'Hanlon went for the kill plunging his sword deep in his enemy's chest, some nearby highlanders observing what was happening closed ranks around their Colonel and carried him away by this time O'Hanlon was so exhausted he was unable to follow. A junior officer seeing his Colonel on foot dismounted and offered him his horse which he gladly accepted a large number of royalists had laid down their arms and were standing around in sullen groups. James gathered them together and confiscated their horses and arms, and then after they swore an oath not to take up arms against America again he sent them on their way. Carts were moving among the dead and wounded and ferrying them to the rear, he spotted the militiaman who had saved his life and spoke to him.

"What is your name is there anything I can do for you?

"Lieutenant Patton sir I'm afraid my knee is shattered but I will be in good hands if you get me to a hospital"

The Colonel spotted an empty cart and called it over.

"I want you to get this officer to the hospital without delay he has a bad injury to his leg"

He took the Lieutenant by the hand,

"I will come and see you in the hospital in a few days"

Alex turned up shortly after.

"James we spotted several boats leaving the point heading for Yorktown, we didn't engage them as they were leaving and we are desperately short of ammunition".

"I have sent a dispatch rider to General Washington with news of our success here, I also took the opportunity to request fresh supplies and ammunition, we are now going to advance to Gloucester point where we will set up camp you keep your guns on the heights to cover us, I don't expect a counter attack but you never know. You can leave a junior officer in charge up there, and you must come and join me I am in need of a good admin officer"

"Surely you can find someone else as an admin officer; you know I have other business to attend to"

"Alex this war will be over soon, maybe in a few days, until then you will remain under my command here at Worcester point, when the war is finished I will join the search for Elizabeth"

The following morning they moved to Worcester Point, all the royalists they encountered were in no mood for a fight and took the oath that they would abstain from further hostile acts against the patriots. Alex organised the 9th into labour groups and built new defences looking out over the York River, they could hear the sounds of battle on the far shore and occasionally some boats made an attempt to cross the half mile distance towards Worcester Point only to be met with a fusillade of gun fire from the point which forced them to turn back. Two days after taking up their positions a huge storm made any river crossing impossible, the soldiers used the time to wash and clean their equipment. Part of the regiment went foraging for supplies with strict instructions to pay for any food or stores they confiscated. The Colonel asked Alex to do him a favour and go to the hospital five miles behind the lines to visit Lieutenant Patton, and make sure he has everything he needs, he set off with the storm still raging. On arrival he asked a hospital orderly if he knew where the Lieutenant was and was directed to a ward reserved for amputees he found him on a cot, he noticed immediately that he had lost one of his legs. Alex was astonished at how well he looked as his leg had been removed only a couple of days ago, he remembered how he nearly died when he lost his arm. Lieutenant the Colonel asked me to visit you and make sure you are comfortable, the Lieutenant reached his hand out with a smile on his face.

"I know he promised to visit, but I never thought he would find time, I am pleased he has sent you, how did you lose the arm, how is the war progressing?

"We have eliminated all opposition on the point, the British Colonel managed to escape in a boat but we know he is severely wounded and with luck he won't survive. I lost my arm at the battle of FORT SULLIVAN a cannon ball hit me in the back of my left shoulder knocking it out of its socket and destroying my arm. I only just survived being at deaths door for several weeks, your quick recovery from the loss of your leg amazes me"

"My doctor is a young man who was the only survivor of an Indian massacre, his father had administered to the ails of all the members of the wagon train and this son helped him, he is now the surgeon to the Mecklenburgh militia, he will be doing the rounds with his beautiful young nurse Louise any moment now"

Five minutes later a young man accompanied by a nurse entered the room, after checking the patient he turned to speak to Alex who was staring at the nurse, he managed to drag his eyes away from her to reply to the doctor who asked how he lost his arm. He gave the doctor a blow by blow account about losing his arm and nearly his life when he finished he asked the doctor how his patient had made such a quick recovery.

"Joe told him how his father had been experimenting with a mixture of opium and laudanum for pain relief, he was well aware that severe pain produced dangerous side effects which could kill most men, the mixture he used caused the patient to become unconscious long enough for him to remove a limb without the patient feeling any pain, he continued administering a mild dose for several days until the patient was stable"

All the time they were talking the nurse was applying a new dressing, with amazing skill for someone so young.

"There now Uncle Arthur how does that feel"

"Wonderful I have little or no pain all I want now is to get home to Charlotte to see Margaret"

"Maybe next week if your recovery continues without any complications"

After the nurse and doctor had departed Alex decided it was time he made his departure, but before going he wanted to ask Arthur a few questions.

"Did I hear that you are from Charlotte, that is where in am heading"

"Yes I have lived there for a few years, I was with the wagon train that got massacred outside Charlotte but luckily for us we had decided to go no further than the town. They were sorely in need of a clergyman and asked the Rev Kerr to stay, he agreed andwe decided to stay too"

Alex began to feel a rush of blood to his head, he managed to stammer out please tell me your name and where you hail from.

"My name is Arthur Patton and I hail from Donegal Pennsylvania, a number of us farmers from that area decided to go south and seek free land as our landlords had become as bad if not worse than the landlords in Ireland"

"Are you the same Arthur Patton who purchased a bonded slave from the market in Wall St about sixteen years ago?"

"You must be speaking about Lizzy she was pregnant at the time and I needed a companion for my wife"

"I am speaking about my wife Elizabeth Williamson we were separated on board ship and I have been searching for her since"

"Then you must be Alexander Williamson she has told me your story many times and she never lost hope that you would be together again one day, my god Alex that young nurse Louise, is your daughter, she is a young woman you should be mighty proud of"

"Please don't tell her about me I want her mother to be present when we are introduced"

"But you have another daughter Fiona, Lizzy had twins"

"Perhaps we will be able to travel to Charlotte together and I will meet them all at the same time"

Alex returned to his unit where the col. informed him Cornwallis had surrendered unconditionally to General Washington, he then told James about the events at the hospital and asked him for leave of absence to return to Charlotte with Lieutenant Patton and Louise. Permission was granted, and he was given his ticket of indefinite leave to join the patriot militia on their return journey to Charlotte.

Chapter 16 Reunion

Alex sent a young gunner to the hospital to find out when the militia were leaving for Charlotte, in the time he had left he trained a young Lieutenant to take over the duties as an admin officer. When the time to part from James came, they drank a jug of moonshine together and vowed to meet up one day after the war. The Mecklenburgh Militia made him welcome, supplying him with food and supplies during the journey. The ambulance wagons carrying six wounded militiamen slowed the convoy down, sadlythe first of the young soldiers Private Allen died on the second day of the journey, he was buried with full military honours and his grave was marked by a stone marker. Joe Craig and his young nurse were in constant demand as several of the walking wounded needed their wounds dressing, and bandages changed. Alex never let Louise out of his sight, but she was too busy to notice him, the militia were under constant harassment by the local Indians sniping at them.

One night time raid saw the militia lose two horses and several weapons, scouts were now sent out to find the Indian village, it was located close to a small stream. The scouts reported it was inhabited by about twenty braves and their families. As the senior officer Alex was asked to try and negotiate a peace treaty with them, he left with a company of militia before dawn the following day. With the help of his soldiers he formed a cordon around the camp and waited for daylight. It was obvious that the largest wigwam was the chiefs, he rode up to it at first light and discharged his weapon, on hearing the shot the braves leapt from their tents brandishing their weapons only to be confronted by mounted soldiers with their weapons loaded and cocked. The chief came running from his tent with his tomahawk in his hand and Alex addressed him.

"You will order your braves to put down their weapons or I will order my men to fire, we have not been provoking you, why are you attacking us?

To Alex's astonishment the chief replied in perfect English.

"You are invading my territory without asking my permission, we served the British for many years and now that they have been defeated we have lost our only source of income".

"We are only passing through and mean no harm; we have no means of paying you if you continue to harass us we will have no alternative but to fight you"

The Chief turned and beckoned to his young son who was standing by the entrance to the tepee to join them.

"This is my son Running Bear one day he will be chief and will need to negotiate treaties with the white man, if you agree to take him to your school and teach him the ways and the language of the white man I will order my braves to let you pass in peace".

Alex readily agreed to this and the young brave after a lengthy goodbye to his parents mounted his pony and joined the soldiers who then returned to the wagons. The chief was true to his word and they continued their journey without incident. As they approached Charlotte Alex's excitement was reaching fever pitch, despite his impatience he was forced to remain with the wagons as they needed all the help they could get to look after the injured men. They entered the small village in the early afternoon, following a meeting with the elders it was agreed that the injured would be looked after by the residents in their own homes. He took young Running Bear to meet the Rev Kerr and explained the promise he had given to the boy's father that he would be educated in the white man's ways; the Rev jumped at the opportunity to convert a future Indian chief to Christianity and took him in to live as part of his family. As soon as he could leave, Alex made his way to the school house where Elizabeth was teaching a class of young pupils. He paused for a minute observing her through the window; his heart was beating so hard he could hear it. He lifted the latch on the door and entered his wife had her back to him writing on the blackboard, she turned on hearing the door to see a one arm man standing there in the shadows, as he moved down the aisle towards her it took a few seconds for her to recognise it was Alex. She screamed his name and rushed down the aisle into his arm with the children looking on in amazement, they held each other in a long passionate embrace before she realised the children were sniggering at them, she paused long enough to dismiss them to their delight. They were reluctant to let go of each other but she pushed him away to arm's length, let me look at you.

"Are you real or are you just a ghost?"

"I'm real alright what's left of me; we must never be parted again Elizabeth promise me"

"I promise! Do you know you have two daughters Louise and Fiona?

"I met up with Louise at the battle of Gloucester Point, she was nursing the wounded when she was pointed out to me, I recognised her straight away as she is so much like you, however I did not make myself known to her as it could have interfered with the important work she was doing"

"Tonight we will become one family for the first time. I cannot wait to introduce you to your daughters for years they have dreamt of the day when we would be together again. You will also meet Arthurs wife Margaret without her we would not have survived they began as my masters but then became my friends. When they entered the house next door it was deserted, Fiona and Edward on hearing the news about Arthur Patton had rushed to the aid station to arrange for his transport home. They set about preparing the sitting room for Arthur, a bed was prepared for him then they sat down together and began to tell each other their stories. Within the hour they heard the cart pull up outside and went to help get Arthur into the house and on to the bed. Margaret was too intent on looking after her man to notice Alex but the twins noticed that their mother was holding on to his one good hand. When Arthur was settled Elizabeth asked everybody to be quiet as she had an announcement to make.

"This handsome man by my side is my long lost husband Alex Williamson, he has spent years tracking me down and was unaware he had two beautiful daughters. The twins rushed to him smothering him in hugs and kisses, they kept repeating over and over again Daddy, Daddy everybody in the room including Arthur in bed was crying. Hours went past; by the time the stories were told it was late into the night, before they all went to bed. For the first time since that night on board The John, Elizabeth and Alex shared a bed. The following day Elizabeth introduced him to his cousin Tom Latimer and they showed him around the small stud farm she had built up with the Pedigree cattle and horses she had brought from Ireland, he was delighted with the quality of the animals which had been cross bred with local stock.

Within the week he visited the offices of The North Carolina Assembly to check the validity of his wife's inheritance. He was assured that the deeds he produced to the land in the Cumberland Valley were legal but it was at present suffering from daily attacks by hostile Indians. Alex was now informed as a disabled officer in the Continental army he would qualify for a land grant in Tennessee should he apply for it. Having studied the army maps of the Cumberland Gap area he applied for a parcel of land adjacent to his wife's inheritance, he was assured this was good land with plenty of water and long grass. On returning home he informed Elizabeth that when his application was approved they would be the proud owners of a thousand acres of good land in Tennessee, and that he would be making plans to travel west to inspect it in the coming months.

"You are going nowhere without me and the twins" said Elizabeth.

"It will be a dangerous journey with hostile Indians threatening us all the way".

"It will be no more dangerous than the journey to Carolina; if you go we all go"

"So be it" said Alex.

They had a family meeting that evening to discuss their plans, the twins insisted that both Joe and Edward be included as they were going nowhere without them. Soon after the meeting had started there came a loud knock on the door, on opening it Alex was faced with an immaculately dressed gentleman who had just alighted from a fine carriage.

"My name is Hugh Williamson I am the surgeon general to the United States and wish to talk to Dr Joe Craig"

"My name is Alex Williamson and I recognise you sir as one of the men who signed the constitution, we are not related but it is a privilege to meet you, young Joe is inside please come in and meet him."

He led the Surgeon General into the kitchen where the meeting was in progress; on introducing him to the assembly he was found a seat.

"My business is with Dr Joe Craig"

"That is me said Joe and these people are my family, you may discuss your business freely in front of them"

"Very well Joe word has come to me what a fine doctor you are, as a new country we need new hospitals with the finest doctors to staff them we intend to build our medical expertise from the ground up. We need to send the best of our young Doctors to France for training in the latest medical practices, the course will last for two years and we will pay all expenses and salaries"

"Joe looked at Louise whose face had gone deathly pale"

"I thank you for this opportunity Sir but Louise has been my nurse throughout the campaign, given the same chance she would make a better Doctor than me"

"I'm sure there would be a place for her if her father would agree"

Joe approached Alex,

"Sir Louise and I have discussed getting married all we need is your permission then we can travel to France as man and wife"

Alex glanced over to his wife who nodded her head with a smile, before he could answer Edward and Fiona stood before him.

"Sir we too want to ask your permission to get married, once again he looked at his wife and again she nodded her head with a broad smile on her face, YES you both have my blessing you may now go ahead and make arrangements"

Hugh Williamson gave a gentle cough and all eyes turned to him,

"I would consider it a great honour to be invited to the double wedding; Alex cannot give two brides away at the same time so if Louise should ask me I would be privileged to give her away to Joe"

Everybody was in agreement with this and Hugh left them to start making their marriage plans.

It was three weeks before the Rev John Kerr could perform the marriage ceremony, when the ceremony was completed all the guests assembled in the school hall to enjoy a large meal which they washed down with quantities of local wine. Early on in the evening while they were still sober Hugh Williamson took Joe out in the garden to talk. He informed him that a place had been found for him and Louise at Pipet-Salpe Triere hospital in Paris. This was the foremost teaching hospital in Europe; they are at the forefront in medical advancement experimenting with Vaccinations to combat small pox. Hugh informed Joe that France was in the throes of a revolution but that it should not affect him as American citizens were well liked and respected by the French people. He informed Joe that he would be accompanying America's three negotiators to the Paris treaty, John Adams, Benjamin Franklyn, and John Jay. These men were tasked with negotiating a peace treaty between England and America. He was instructed to be in Boston in four weeks' time accompanied by Louise where an American ship would carry them to France.

"All arrangements have been made for you both to study under the finest medical brains in the world for two years, you will then return home where a brand new teaching hospital will be built for you to pass on your newly acquired knowledge and skills to young students wishing to become doctors and surgeons"

The two men shook hands and took leave of each other Joe returned to the festivities while Hugh Williamson began the long journey home. The newly married couple spent their first night together in Harrison's hotel and neither left their rooms until late the following day. Louise and Joe decided to remain there until it was time to catch the stage to Boston while Fiona and Edward were found room in the Family house. Mr and Mrs Craig spent all their spare time with the family prior to their departure; Fiona and Louise were broken hearted when the time came for them to part two years would seem like a lifetime

Soon after their departure Alex had a meeting with the rest of his immediate family, they discussed the possibility of moving south west to set up home on the substantial lands they now owned in Tennessee. The family were in agreement and Alex suggested inviting his cousin Tom Latimer and the young Indian boy Running Bear who had now been baptised and given the Christian name Shay Harrison to accompany them if they would agree, Tom to look after the horses and cattle and the young Indian boy Shay would be invaluable in negotiating with any unfriendly Cherokee they met on the way. It turned out both were pleased to be included in the venture so work started immediately on recovering the Conestoga wagon from where it had been stored. It would require a new canvas top; the wheels had deteriorated and needed replacing, numerous timber planks where showing signs of rot and needed replacing Tom was allocated the job of buying eight strong horses and repairing or replacing pieces of the harness. By the following April everything was in readiness, and they waited for the next wagon train calling at Charlotte for supplies. Luckily for them it was group of sixteen wagons most of the families were from Ulster but the wagon master was an Italian man named Fabrizio Federico he was delighted to have them join them and suggested they call him Fab like the rest of the party.

Elizabeth was devastated when Margaret informed her they would be staying in Charlotte; she pointed out that Arthur with only one leg would not be fit enough for such a dangerous trek, everyone agreed with her. The day came for them to depart and Alex steered his team into line. The Rev John Kerr gave a short ceremony and a blessing to the entire wagon train before they set off on their long hazardous journey.

Printed in Great Britain
by Amazon